THE REAL HOUSEWIVES OF THE BIBLE

OF THE BIBLE

THERESA V. WILSON

Writers in the Marketplace™ Press Subsidiary of VMAssociates, Inc.

The Real Housewives of the Bible by Theresa V. Wilson Copyright ©2020

ISBN: [Ebook] 978-0-615-30582-0
ISBN: [Trade Paperback] 978-1-7356409-0-7

Or by writing author at:

Director, Book Marketing
VMAssociates, Inc
P.O. Box 47182
Windsor Mill, MD 21244

Cover Designed by: J.L. Woodson, Woodson Creative Studio
Interior Design & Formatting: DHBonner Virtual Solutions, LLC
Developmental Editing by: Lissa Woodson
Content Editing by: Janice Allen
Beta Reader Consultant: Debra J. Mitchell

THE REAL HOUSEWIVES OF THE BIBLE

THERESA V. WILSON

THERESA WILSON BOOKS
MOVING FROM VISION TO PRINT

To John Douglas (JD), my husband, my love, best friend, navigator, covering and first point of contact when developing writing ideas; to my beautiful, strong and authentic daughter, Donielle. Your positive attitude, high energy, and consistent "we can make it" attitude has made me proud. I will always cherish how close we've become. To my mom, Ireatha, a quiet strength who has always been there for me, and without whom I would not exist; and to my crazy step-daughter, Shayna, who keeps me laughing during our hours of conversation. So very glad we connected.

CONTENTS

ACKNOWLEDGMENTS

Giving all glory and honor to my God, the big "G," the Source of all resources I needed to finish a work begun in 2016.

Special acknowledgement to the *Writers in the Marketplace Christian Consumer Readers* (CCR) group members Pastor Rosalind Schwind, Torre Parker, Donielle Rooks, and Joseph and Kathy Lundari. The value of your insight, prayers, critique, feedback, and written commentaries cannot be measured. You confirmed the greatest lesson I learned in this process. To have like-minded people put the final eye on your work is the difference between the chariots of fire and a flickering flame. To Lissa Woodson, who God assigned to me for a season.

NOTE TO THE READER

The stories in this book are speculative Christian fiction. It does not, in any way, replace or rewrite the irrefutable word of God. This means several descriptions of biblical characters, situations, and relationships were created to fit the narrative. The biblical scenery is the same, with the stories taking place on the continent of Africa focused on the people whose descendants are Israelites. The story line was adapted based on authentic historical figures, with some of the narrative content infused with a dialogue of what could have been behind the scenes events and circumstances, that may have influenced their decisions and choices that change the course of history.

The idea for this book was first roughed in 2016. I started a draft but, like many of my fellow authors, I allowed myself to be distracted with other projects. The unfinished thoughts rested on a flash drive—forgotten. In 2020, sequestered by COVID 19, I rediscovered my initial draft. The rest is history.

It is my sincere hope this book inspires you to engage the scriptures and follow other Christian fiction writers who exhibit a heart to explore, create, and share works that expand the imagination. Thank you, enjoy the journey.

STORY ONE: HOUSEWIFE OF CANAAN: BATHSHEBA, URIAH AND KING DAVID

CHAPTER 1

"Even men and women who love God can yield to temptations that result in bitter consequences to themselves and others."
— Author Unknown

The afternoon sun streamed through the lace covered windows, illuminating the soft lavender and pink cushioned chairs. A warm breeze caressed the water lilies perched in a blue vase located on the small bedroom side table. "This is so exciting," Bathsheba shouted from her closet, while shuffling through a maze sheath dresses and scarfs. "I can't believe this. Father's home and Shabel will be here this evening to ask him if we can be married."

Johanna, Bathsheba's closest friend, listened, breathed deep, grabbed a chair, sat and watched as dress after dress came flying from the closet, creating a pile on the bed.

"Good grief girl. Make a selection. I'm hungry and can smell lunch." Johanna grunted, rubbed her stomach, and yawned. "So, your dad met Shabel for the one hundredth time, on his last visit home. And, for the one hundredth time, Shabel hesitated approaching him." Shifting in the chair, while stretching her head toward the closet, Johanna continued. "Tell me, what makes you think he's going to get up the nerve to ask for your hand this time?"

Bathsheba made sure the last dress she tossed out of the closet, hit girlfriend on the head. Appearing in the doorway, she leaned on the closet door frame, and eyed her friend.

"It wasn't a hundred times," she chided, brows knitted in a frown. "Maybe ninety-nine." They burst out laughing, as Bathsheba's long curly dark brown hair fell forward, covering her hazel brown eyes.

"Seriously," Johanna continued. Shabel needs to get moving on talking to your poppa. You never know whether his next time away from home will last three months, six months or longer. I've been hearing gossip. A lot is going on along the borders."

Holding an armload of dresses, Bathsheba flopped on the bed. "Yeah, I know. I just didn't want Shabel to approach when dad's in the military mindset. I love him but, in that mode, there's no room for frivolous issues." Bathsheba grabbed one of her dresses, and started fluffing its edges. "Unfortunately, my getting married is a frivolous issue for him." She tossed the pile of dresses she had been holding on the bed, squeezed her eyes shut, and chuckled.

"Now, if I was a son, approaching him to discuss my plans to join one of the legions of the King, that would grab his attention. In fact, he'd pull up a chair, and spend the entire evening with me."

With half a laugh, Johanna hugged her friend. "Personally, I'm glad you weren't a boy." Both girls giggled again.

Bathsheba was so engaged in conversation with Johanna, she didn't notice her mother standing in the doorway, listening, and observing. "Well," Lydia offered reaching for the pile of cloths on the bed. "Can I assume you're selecting something to wear for the day, or are you moving out?"

Bathsheba, watched her mother cross the room. She could usually gauge the vibe to expect when greeting her dad by her mother's behavior. It was hard to judge this time. She raised her hand in greeting.

"Not moving out yet, mom. Remember, Shabel will be visiting for dinner, and I was just trying to find the right dress for the occasion."

Lydia smoothed her hands over the dress materials. "Occasion you say? Well, I'm sure whatever it is, you'll look stunning as always. In the meantime, your father wants to see you."

Bathsheba cocked a brow in surprise. "Now, before lunch?" "Yes." Lydia replied, and took her girlfriend's arm. "Johanna and I will go to the veranda and sit by the pool for a few moments, enjoying the sun, while waiting for you and your father to join us."

Bathsheba automatically smoothed her hair and straightened the invisible wrinkles from her dress.

Lydia smiled. "You look fine. Now go visit with your father so we can eat!" She said with a broad smile. Almost too bright and cheerful for her daughter's liking.

Bathsheba prepared to leave, giving Johanna a side eye. They had just discussed how the appearance of her father could mean peace and quiet, with no issues, or two or three days of the household in turmoil, and nerves on edge. In addition, her father was known for giving unreasonable orders, and offering endless lectures about the proper way things are supposed to run. His focus, ensuring efficiency. Rechecking her scarf, she looked at her mom.

"You know, I feel nervous about going to see father, but I remember things weren't always this way. As a child, I couldn't wait to hear that Eliam was home. He was larger than life to me then. He was kinder, more caring and playful. I was his little girl."

Looking at her mom, she paused. "Did I ever tell you, on several of my trips with him, father even let me play in the corners of the great hall in the palace, while he and grandfather Ahithophel attended council meetings? Yep, I was his girl until I grew older."

"I often wonder what it would have been like if I had been a boy."

Lydia patted Bathsheba's hand and gave her a quick kiss. "Your father loves you. He loves us both," her mother said almost like she was trying to convince herself. "He arrived late last night. It was a bit of a surprise, as he usually sends his messenger ahead for advance planning. Now go."

Taking Bathsheba's hand and pointing Johanna to the exit, Lydia signaled it was time to leave. "Your father has some news to share with you, baby. It concerns you...your future."

Bathsheba yanked her hand. "Well, I'm certainly looking forward to this, because he certainly has very little knowledge about what's been going on in my immediate past."

Lydia stepped between Bathsheba and the exit. "Give your father a chance. Don't go meet with him assuming you won't like what he'll say, especially since you have no idea what it's all about. Everything he does is for our good, even when we don't understand it completely. I suggest you adjust your attitude before it gets you in trouble."

Bathsheba backed into the room, shut her eyes, and gritted her teeth. Lydia followed, and closed the door. "Okay, mother. Here we go again." She whispered, ignoring Johanna standing a few feet on the other side of the door. "What is it this time? What new chores am I being assigned? Where does he plan to ship me to expand my intellectual horizons? I know it can't be battlefield duties, cause I'm not a man—tough luck."

Lydia didn't answer, lowered her eyes, and squirmed under the intense scrutiny. "All I can tell you is your father has the details."

Before Bathsheba could comment further, her handmaid knocked and entered. "Miss Bathsheba, ma'am, your father has sent me. He bids you to come to his office." Bathsheba didn't acknowledge her existence. She turned, walk onto her balcony, leaned over the stone wall divider, and began tapping the base of the wall with her foot, while pretending to concentrate on the scenery below—as if no one was around.

The handmaid stood near the balcony entrance. "Now ma'am. He asked that you come now."

Bathsheba stood erect, and nodded. "Yes, thank you." Her handmaid bowed and left the room. In silence, she brushed her hair into a quick ponytail, tied the headscarf, and smoothed her dress in place once again. With a forced smile to her friend, and a penetrating glare at her mother, Bathsheba tossed her head and left the room without a word.

It was a long walk to her father's office. Several times she paused, looking around for a distraction that would give her an excuse to delay her arrival. Finding none, she kept walking. Reaching her destination, Bathsheba took a deep breath, opened the door, and entered. "You called for me, father?" She said, while searching for a place to sit. Still holding the door handle, she scanned the room. Her gaze fell on the familiar face of Uriah, the soldier, standing at attention, on the other side of the door. Clean shaven, with close hair cropped to accommodate his uniform helmet, this tall, neatly attired man stood like a statue awaiting orders. Ignoring him, she returned to her father.

"I'm sorry, if I'm late?" She offered, as a way to start a conversation. Eliam smiled. No emotion, just a quick smile. Her heart sank.

"Yes, daughter. Come in. I have some news to discuss with you." From past experience, Bathsheba knew the fact that he hadn't moved from behind the desk was not a good sign. This was definitely going to be one of those do as I say, not as I do sessions. Bathsheba walked across the room, and perched on the edge of one of the comfortable plush caramel goat skin chairs. She postured as if she were attending a business meeting. Uriah, still standing at the door, was staring, so she loosened the scarf and let her hair fall forward to cover most of her face—wishing it was a veil.

"Daughter," Elaim spoke, while continuing to adjust the pile of papers on his desk. "I've decided it is time to let you know the plans I have for your future. I've arranged for you to be married to someone I feel would be good for you, and your future. I've spoken to one of my best officers, who has agreed this would make a perfect match." Bathsheba cleared her throat, but remained silent.

Eliam raised his hand and pointed toward the office door. "Now I know you already know Uriah and ..." Before he could continue, Bathsheba raised her hand like she was in a tutoring session trying to get her teacher's attention.

"Father, please stop. You can't mean this. You have been away for months, so you're not aware of what's going on in my life. A lot has happened in your absence."

Bathsheba stood and approached her father. "I am going to marry Shabel. You know him. He comes from a well-respected, influential family. I know him and I love him."

Normally short on words, and with low tolerance for explaining his decisions, Elaim placed both elbows on the desk, fingers interlocking, holding his chin. One heavy brow slanted in strong disapproval. Bathsheba grew quiet. Her father leaned closer, maintaining full eye contact.

"As a way to reduce any more of these emotional outbursts, and make my decision clear, let me provide for you, Bathsheba, a brief overview of how I came to this decision, and what will be the next steps."

Elaim arose from his chair, moved away from the desk, and pointed for Bathsheba to sit. "During my last military campaign, I had several discussions with Uriah about his future. These discussions eventually included you, and my arranging your marriage." Smiling, he walked to the door of his office, and placed a hand on Uriah's shoulder. "It's not like you don't know Uriah. In fact, I thought you had a very cordial relationship."

Uriah shifted his stance, smiled at Eliam then looked at Bathsheba. His smile disappeared under the hard glare she gave him.

Elaim continued. "I am very proud of this young man, and his rapid movement within the ranks, having already been promised to join the king's Mighty Men." Rubbing his hands, he looked at Bathsheba. "I am very pleased with this arrangement. As for Shabel, from what I remember, he's a nice young man, but this is a military family. I plan that you marry a military man."

Eliam returned to his desk. "With that being said, arrangements for this covenant were finalized a few days ago. I intend for the ceremony to take place shortly—within the week—as you will need to move and get settled in your new home, before Uriah's next campaign."

Bathsheba dropped her head and sat very still, listening, as her life was rearranged.

"Uriah is a good man, with a promising future," Eliam continued, his heart stopping gaze narrowed on his daughter. "He is steady, dependable, and conscientious and I have full confidence in his integrity. He will make a good husband for you. I am firm with my decision. You will move forward with this union to take place within these next five days."

Five days!

"That way you can travel with him to the temporary assignment in Damascus," he continued, ignoring her silence. "You will also have time to adjust to married life before the next move. This is my plan that you will follow to the letter." At the conclusion of his comments, her father walked to his office door, and escorted Uriah to Bathsheba's chair.

"Come, son. Join us," Elaim said, as he stepped aside to allow the man, dressed in military garb, to become part of the gathering. Uriah bowed toward Bathsheba, then stood at attention. Elaim threw Bathsheba a warning glance.

Ignoring Uriah, Bathsheba approached her father, touching his arm while speaking.

"Why are we rushing this decision, father? You have been away for several months. My life didn't stop in that time. I fell in love. I hope you understand, and think it only fair that you take my feelings into account when making decisions about my life."

Bathsheba felt her father's arm stiffened while she was speaking. When he glared at her, she stopped, lowered her hand and reclaimed her seat. "Father, I don't question your choice or decision." *Lies. I'm questioning everything.* "But, if this is to be, I always dreamed I could choose my husband, and plan my wedding. I can see now that trying to convince you Shabel is a better choice, is not an option for me. I will, of course, obey this decision, but it is still a special event."

With tears flowing, Bathsheba look at her father. *Desperate times require desperate measures. If she could only delay this insanity.*

"With less than a week to prepare, it just makes me sad that I won't be able to celebrate this marriage with my friends in attendance."

The two men exchanged glances. Uriah shifted then returned to his original position near the door. He took several steps forward. "Sir," he interjected while ignoring Bathsheba's glare. "By your permission, I will take my leave while you work on these details, as planned."

Eliam nodded approval. Uriah bowed to Bathsheba, saluted Eliam, and left the room. Bathsheba followed Uriah's grand exit, taking in his cool distant look, and practiced behavior of bowing to her with the same indifference he would offer a stranger. Bathsheba turned to her father.

"Father, I know Uriah has been around forever, and this may seem like a simple arrangement, but it's just not that simple for me."

Eliam, eyes cold and piercing, sat on his brown goat skin arm chair, behind the desk, and locked gazes with his daughter. "Bathsheba, I will speak on this subject one final time. The marriage has been arranged. I chose for you a good man whose integrity is unquestioned. You will marry within the week. This you will do in obedience to me." With that comment, Eliam returned his attention to the paperwork the King had requested be reviewed. He never looked up again.

Bathsheba's life had dramatically changed. In a few short moments, she lost her choice of husband—Shabel was tossed aside—and had to accept she was entering a new life as a military wife. She would leave her comfortable and familiar surroundings behind, to follow a man she didn't know, and live in areas of the region selected based on her new husband's assignments. Bathsheba stood, wiped her face and turned to leave.

"Bathsheba," her father said to her retreating back. "No need to communicate with Shabel. I will send him a message. Focus on preparing for your new life. Put this all behind you."

Bathsheba did not acknowledge her father's words. She closed the door to her father's office and her old life.

CHAPTER 2

Two days before the abbreviated wedding ceremony, Bathsheba folded the last of her dresses and glanced at the array of sandals that would be left behind. She was certain, based on who she was marrying, there would be little use for a variety of footwear and fancy garments. The final accessories were tossed in the baggage and secured with a lock. Only by outward appearance was she ready to face this uncertain future.

At mid-afternoon, a few hours before supper, she stepped onto her balcony overlooking the family's expansive, colorful gardens. This had been her refuse for years. Because her suite was toward the back end of the house, the balcony was a little larger than her parents, and she had a back staircase leading to the veranda and pool. "I have to leave all this behind," she mumbled.

While staring at the landscape, her handmaid entered to take several of her packed belongings to the lower level. "Ma'am, we were told you would be leaving soon after the ceremony, and we have been instructed to ensure your belongings were in place, ready for transport." As the handmaid opened the door to leave, her mother entered.

Bathsheba was relieved to learn she and her new husband would not stay at the family compound overnight, in a special cottage, as would have been the custom. It was a relief to know she would not have to perform any wifely duties—at least for the moment. They would travel immediately to his next assignment in Damascus, where he would be stationed for several months before a planned reassignment, that would enable them to live in Jerusalem.

"Ma'am," her handmaid interrupted. "You have a visitor." Bathsheba took one last look at the peaceful scenery, then walked away from her special place on the balcony. "Now what?" she spoke aloud, not necessarily to anyone.

The handmaid took a pointed interest in tidying up the bed. "It's your fiancée, ma'am. He requests you join him in your father's den, if you are able. He's alone ma'am."

Bathsheba threw her hands in the air. "This boring excuse for a man wants to talk to me now," she mumbled. She tossed a scowling look at her handmaid, who immediately bowed, and left the room. Bathsheba paced in front of the bedroom door for some minutes contemplating her next move. She checked her hair and performed additional personal care tasks in slow motion. To further extend the wait, on the way to her meeting, Bathsheba took a detour through the gardens. She noticed her mother standing near one of the chairs. Lydia greeted her daughter with a wave.

"Honey, I know this is a bit overwhelming but it's for the best." Bathsheba studied, with piercing scrutiny, this woman she called mother. She sighed and took her hand. "Please. No more talk from you about what's good for me. I just want to get this over with." She turned and walked away.

* * *

Uriah was standing at the window, observing the workmen constructing the temporary arch to be used for the wedding ceremony. Preoccupied with those construction details, he didn't notice the door had opened. Bathsheba kicked a chair to gain his attention. Uriah whirled around, with his hand positioned over his sword.

"Bathsheba," he started, then cleared his throat. "I thought we should have a few moments together. I realize everything is sudden, but well, it's not like we don't know each other. Once you have time to adjust to the situation, I'm sure things will be fine between us. "You're a fine young lady and—"

Bathsheba raised both hands toward Uriah. "Please stop." She sneered as she focused a cold stare at her future husband. "You've done well for yourself, Uriah," she said while strutting around the room. "Marrying more than affluence, you're also inheriting promising opportunities, with my grandfather one of King's Chief Advisors, and my father assigned as one of his Mighty Men."

Bathsheba moved closer to Uriah, taking deliberate slow-motion steps. "I hear you're also due to join the ranks of the inner circle, so clearly your connections are paying off royally." Bathsheba curled her lip and tossed her hair back, while grunting as she looked her betrothed up and down. "But that wasn't enough was it?"

Uriah eyes blazed like torches. This was a different kind of battlefield for him. He approached Bathsheba, using long strides, and an unrelenting stare. "You know Bathsheba," Uriah growled, "I patiently remained at my post, in the corner of the room the other day, because I felt it was important for your father to handle his daughter, and her female rantings about what she wanted." He grabbed a pillow from a nearby chair and threw it across the room.

Bathsheba started for the door, but Uriah blocked her way. "Look, I like and respect your father, but I had absolutely no interest in experiencing a formal wedding ceremony." Bathsheba crossed her arms and rolled her eyes. Uriah glued his eyes on her, until the arms relaxed and dropped to her side.

He took one step back and continued. "Your father is my mentor and, after lengthy discussions, we agreed it was time that I had a wife. You fit the role, and I agreed to the arrangement. That is all."

Bathsheba walked over to the window and scanned the beautiful lush gardens. She almost enjoyed the view, except for the ugly ceremonial arch standing in the way. "Well, that's a nice, neat package. The only thing missing was my input and agreement."

Uriah ignored the comment and continued. "I plan, and he agrees, that a simple legal covenant and small ceremony would work, so I can move on to the business of leading my men. You, my dear, will fulfill your role as my wife. I can be a good husband for you but, let's be clear I won't put up with attitudes."

Uriah followed Bathsheba to the window, remaining quiet. It was several days since the exchange in her father's office. Now, he needed to take control of this 'spit fire' or he was destined for a miserable relationship. He stood very close behind his future bride. "I don't care whether or not you love me, but you will respect me. You will *look* the part and *live* the part.

Bathsheba threw her head back and laughed. "Well, that was some speech. Feel better now?"

Uriah grabbed Bathsheba's arms and brought her close to him. She struggled, but his grip was strong as he turned her chin to face him. "You will be my bride. This is a fact. The arrangements are set and all preliminary details finalized." He leaned in so there was only inches between her lips and his. "You can fight this arrangement, *my love*," he continued—emphasizing every word, while his heart- stopping, piercing eyes show how he felt. "Or you can resolve to be a dutiful bride, and I will treat you well. Hear me, if you cause me any embarrassment, I will make your life miserable." Uriah whispered.

Bathsheba regained her composure. She did not want her father to suspect there had been a confrontation with her future husband. An embarrassment for Eliam would only make matters worse for her. She relaxed her body, and surrendered to Uriah's grip. Gazing first at his hand, her eyes move across his broad shoulders upward, until they rested on his eyes, bearing down on her. Bathsheba reached for his chin.

"You swept into my life without warning. Though we have passed each other many times in past years, never once have we recognized the other's existence." Uriah relaxed his body and waited.

Bathsheba gently massaged his brow and the side of his face. "In less than two days' time, my life abruptly changed and I find myself packing, without having yet one close contact with the man I am told I would marry. And today, that first contact is a hostile takeover demonstrated by a firm, angry grip, and a warning. I know you don't believe in sweeping a girl off her feet, but could we try again?"

Uriah gently pushed Bathsheba far enough away to look more closely at her face. "What, have we a change of heart, my love?"

Bathsheba moved in and rested her head on his shoulders. "I want to be a good wife, Uriah, but I need help."

Uriah loosened his grip, rubbed her arm with his thumb, kissed her on the cheek, then stepped back, and bowed. "As you wish Bathsheba. We shall start again."

Bathsheba sighed. "I know you have many duties to complete before our wedding ceremony takes place, and I want you to know how much I appreciate the time you took to see me today."

Uriah let a faint smile cross his lips. Bathsheba slowly moved across the floor, and opened the door to exit. She looked back long enough to catch Uriah watching, before she closed the door behind her. "Think on that soldier boy," she murmured, and went to her room.

* * *

"I will miss you," Johanna said to her friend while helping with last minute packing. Bathsheba smiled and hugged her friend, then she sat on her bed one final time. "You know, I was able to use a few of my mother's tactics a few days ago, that I know will help me get through this, while I plan a proper revenge. I don't know how, but I plan Uriah lives to regret his decision to marry me."

Johanna shook her head. "Try to make the best of it. Unlike the guys, we have no control over our lives. Don't make yourself unhappy trying."

Bathsheba smiled. "Yes, he won this battle. That's clear. But I will win the war against this self-righteous, pompous, toy soldier." Throwing the last of her clothes in a small satchel, she opened the door and hugged her girlfriend. "Come. The last guest of my impromptu marriage ceremony must be gone by now. Join me in the garden. Let's have a cup of wine, just you and me Sis. A toast to my future. It beats crying."

CHAPTER 3

Dry weather, then rain, and mud. All the best weather extremes, in one place, and at the wrong time. Shaking dust from her sandals, Bathsheba entered the cottage she and Uriah shared. After a few short steps, she entered their combined dining and guest visiting area. The servants kept the room well supplied with fresh flowers daily. To resolve space challenges they faced, Bathsheba purchased a tall decorative cedar wood room divider, creating the transition from eating to entertaining.

The handmaid followed Bathsheba carrying fruits, vegetables, fish and fresh meat from the local market. "Ma'am the room for dining is so beautiful. You did such a wonderful job."

Bathsheba chuckled. "Yeah. A lot of wasted effort on that project. Your master is never home, so we never have guests visit to enjoy it."

They made a quick left and entered a small kitchen area supplied with only the basic needs for meal preparation. Living with her parents, she never ventured to the local marketplace. Except for special occasions, that was the job for servants. Unfortunately, with this new military assignment, shopping became another way of escaping boring daily routines.

The newlyweds had been living in Damascus for the last two months. Uriah was off on yet another military campaign and there was no projected time for his return. She tried to make the best of her situation by connecting with other military wives. Elena, another military wife and Bathsheba first met in the marketplace. They found they had a lot in common—including a hate for military wife life—and became inseparable. From shopping excursions to late evenings at each other's home sipping wine, while commiserating about their lives, these two women developed creative activities to escape the boredom of military wife life, which they soon shared with other wives.

One evening, they relaxed on the veranda, enjoying the cool breeze, wine, and a platter of grapes, melon, and apples. Elena stretched, smoothed her hair and leaned forward to adjust her position. "You know we're running out of ideas for our wife gatherings. We're stuck on this military compound. It's not like we can run into town or tour the countryside."

Bathsheba nodded and reached for another piece of fruit. "True but the rules are for our protection, Elena. They can't let anybody in and they can't very well protect us, if we are out gallivanting in some unsecured area. I agree walking around the compound is no treat, but we'll just have to keep creating ideas and pushing these boring women to join in. "Now, let's focus on our next gathering with the ladies. I already have the handmaids squeezing pomegranates for coloring. This should be a fun event."

Elena laughed. "You're right. Let's do it." Bathsheba and her friend achieved their greatest accomplishment that night. The guests complemented them on an enjoyable evening. The papyrus canvas, and paint brushes made of twigs and leaves from oak trees were a hit.

Everyone relaxed and ate until there was nothing left. Bathsheba finally found her niche as a military wife.

* * *

Several days after the success of her military wife gathering, Bathsheba returned home, after completing a shopping spree for another special celebration. Her parents were visiting. In spite of the cool farewell Bathsheba displayed when departing on the marital journey, she was excited receiving the message that both parents would be visiting, and should arrive within the day.

Bathsheba was relaxing in her room, with Sasha brushing her hair, when the commotion of horses entering the front entrance leading to their home snatched her attention.

She turned to Sasha. "Help me get ready. I guess my mother and father arrived early."

Grabbing a sheath dress and sandals, she rushed to finish dressing, then hurried to greet them. Bathsheba approached the reception area while still tying the scarf around her hair. She stopped midway. Uriah was standing in the doorway.

Bathsheba dropped her arms. "What are you doing here? I mean, this is such a surprise."

Neither Uriah nor Bathsheba moved. No attempt at physical contact. Instead, Bathsheba entered and circled the room like a captured animal. "So how long can I expect your visit this time?" she almost whispered.

Uriah's eyes rolled skyward. "I will stay as long as it takes to do what I need to do. Right now, I need to make sure my men are properly cared for, then I will clean up, and prepare for my in-law's visit."

Bathsheba stop moving, and shot a disgusted look in his direction. "What do you mean? Are you saying you already knew about my parents' visit before I did?" Head tilted slightly to the side, she leaned forward. "So, all of you planned this visit in advance, right?" She waited for a reply. He stood motionless and said nothing.

Bathsheba chuckled. "I should have known. What's this gathering really all about? Why are they coming and why are you here?"

Uriah breathed heavily and approached his wife. "Bathsheba, once again you assume details belong to you. Not so. Your father and I communicate on a regular basis. When the information results in a need for you to be informed, it happens."

He plucked a flower from its root in a nearby pot and pulled the petals one by one, letting them fall to the floor. "You were notified that your parents would be visiting. Your responsibility, as my wife, whenever there are guests, is to prepare for their arrival. Because of the nature of their visit, I decided I would be present, at least for a short while, during this time."

Bathsheba was stunned at his response. Uriah had stepped into the role of son to her father. She was now an afterthought. Clearly there was more news to share but, for the moment, only three of the four people affected were aware of the specifics.

"I guess, by your statement, I am not to be informed about this announcement until all the players are in the room."

Uriah was silent. Bathsheba threw her hands in the air, and left the room.

By early evening Bathsheba's parents arrived and settled in their guest quarters to refresh after their journey. Bathsheba was not available to greet them. With dishes in place, and the aroma of food in the air, the parents were seated on either side of Uriah at the dining table. The atmosphere was tense, as they awaited Bathsheba's arrival.

Uriah turned so he could have a clear view of his father-in-law. "So, Sir, how was the trip? Did my men provide well for your comfort?" Eliam nodded agreement, turned to his wife, and patted her hand. "We were treated very well. A good trip. Your men are well trained."

Usually Bathsheba's mother remains quiet, following the unwritten rule of women being seen but not heard in mixed company. Today, however, was different. They received a cold reception on their arrival, with the servants sending messages that her daughter was unavailable until dinner. Lydia wanted to know what was wrong. During a brief silence, she turned to Uriah and blurted a question.

"It's only been a few months, but how's married life?"

Eliam placed his hand firmly on his wife's hand. He squeezed so hard, she winced. She bowed her head, avoiding eye contact.

Uriah cleared his throat and responded to his father-in-law. "As you know, Sir, I have been away these past few weeks. Not much time for husband duties. I only just arrived today to ensure I did not miss your visit."

Uriah reached for the platter of fruit, smiled, and offered it to his mother-in-law. "I fear I spoiled this reunion a bit. You see, Bathsheba was a little put out that I knew of your visit, and that there was a purpose. Apparently, she doesn't like surprises," he chuckled. "I still have much to learn about my bride." Looking at the door, he offered, "it appears she may be delayed a few more minutes for dinner, so why don't we serve our plates? Sir, would you bless the food?"

As soon as blessings concluded, the door opened and Bathsheba appeared, her handmaid in attendance. "Greetings family," she said unsmiling, as she moved from mother to father, giving each an air kiss then sat at the end of the table, opposite Uriah.

Seated, she looked at Uriah, unsmiling. "May I have a cup, no a goblet of wine. This promises to be an interesting evening." Her handmaid poured the wine, bowed, and left the room.

Uriah looked sideways at Bathsheba's father and mother. "It's apparent we will not be able to wait until after the meal for our announcement. I thought my plan would fare better than it did, and, for this, I apologize."

Uriah narrowed his gaze on Bathsheba. "Your father has been my mentor longer than you have been my wife. I honor him and trust his advice and counsel. This relationship has afforded me the opportunity to be rewarded many times over with favor in assignments throughout the region." Uriah arose from his seat at the head table and stood beside his father-in-law's chair, maintaining eye contact with his wife. He placed both hands on the table and leaned forward.

"I have also, because of your father, found favor with the king, as I have been officially designated as one of his mighty men. This appointment is an honor every soldier seeks, and the wife of a soldier should be proud to hear." He stood straight and rigid. "Tonight, was supposed to be a surprise for you, my wife, in that I have now been reassigned to Jerusalem."

Bathsheba's mouth dropped open and eyes widened in disbelief. Crossing her arms, she scanned the room, moving from Uriah to her mother then father. "Well, how nice," she responded, and did not say another word.

Eliam and Lydia looked at each other, then back to Uriah. The handmaids had entered the room to clear away dishes but, after observing the scene, quietly backed away and left the area.

Bathsheba shot a disgusted glance at her father. "So, what does this entail, and how does it affect me?"

Uriah, walked back to his chair. "It means we are moving. I will be assigned duties around Jerusalem, in addition to overseeing various military campaigns in the region." Silence.

Eliam addressed his daughter. "Actually, I am surprised at your response, my dear. I thought you would be happy to reside in Jerusalem."

Bathsheba rolled her eyes and smirked. "Really. How would you know what makes me happy?"

Uriah cleared his throat, and ignored the comment. "Because the assignment begins immediately, your mother is here to help with packing and moving. I have to leave tomorrow to set up the offices, issue new assignments to my leaders, and prepare for the next campaign."

Uriah arose from the table and, with a disapproving gleam in his eyes, stood by Bathsheba's chair. "Your father will travel with me to assist in the transition."

Bathsheba started to protest, but Uriah placed his hand on her shoulder. "You will prepare to move my sweet. That is all." Bathsheba scanned the table. Lydia fiddled with the wine cup in silence.

Elaim gave her a rueful smile. "Bathsheba, your husband received a great honor in this appointment. He made a decision which means you both move to Jerusalem, which will be good for your future. As his wife, you are to obey."

Uriah squeezed his wife's shoulder. "Now. Let's have dinner, shall we?" Bathsheba remained silent. Defeated again.

CHAPTER 4

To Bathsheba's relief, Uriah spent the next two days sleeping in the tents with his troops instead of trying to demand his marital rights. He made the excuse that there were many details requiring his attention before leaving.

By the third day, Uriah and her father had left for Jerusalem. Bathsheba shipped her mother home soon after. She had no interest in forcing conversations, and little or no need for company. Bathsheba loved her mother but didn't need her now. With four handmaids and security guards assigned by Uriah, Bathsheba joined a large caravan, and traveled from the plateau of Damascus to the hills of Jerusalem.

As the wife of one who was part of the king's mighty men, Bathsheba enjoyed all the comforts of royalty on her journey. Her tents were set apart and well-guarded, the food specially prepared. Uriah, as a peace offering, promised a whole new wardrobe when they arrived. Despite the long journey, she was enjoying the adventure. Her only regret was traveling toward her husband instead away from him.

The morning of the last day's travel, Bathsheba was awakened by a loud commotion taking place not far from her tent. One of the handmaids rushed in, with her hands in the air, screaming.

"Ma'am, Ma'am, the king! King David is passing by with his troops."

Bathsheba was amused at how excited her maid appeared. She was definitely curious, especially since she heard how tall, handsome, and strong he was. Still struggling to secure both robe and sandals, she finally joined her handmaid a few yards beyond the tent entrance. The cheering crowd was almost deafening. People were screaming and running toward a tall figure riding in a magnificent, well-designed chariot. Because of the distance, and the scarfs, shawls, and flowers the people were frantically waving in the air, she could not see his face.

Bathsheba watched the crowd's display of affection for a few moments longer before returning to the privacy of her tent. Upon entering, Uriah was standing in the center area, shield in one hand and helmet in another. On his right side was a gleaming sword; from waist up was a shining metal breastplate armor of copper, glistening from the light of the sun beam that seemed to be focused on every part of his body.

Bathsheba had never really paid attention to her husband, when suited up in his military garb. Looking at him now, she had to admit, he was impressive. But then he blew it by opening his mouth.

"I am here to escort you into the gates of Jerusalem," he announced proudly as he clicked his heels and bowed.

In spite of his formal greeting, Bathsheba smiled. Her handmaid quietly left the area. At that moment, Bathsheba decided now was a good time to become Uriah's wife, hoping some affection between them would somehow make life more bearable.

Bathsheba opened her robe, letting it slowly fall to the floor, and walked over to her husband. She was wearing nothing but a thin shear gown. She wrapped her arms around his neck and spoke softly.

"Uriah, my husband, can we not have a better greeting than that," she whispered. "I am your wife. I accept this. Let us begin this marriage again today.

Uriah dropped his shield, grabbed his wife and kissed her long and hard. Bathsheba pulled him closer to her, an instant hunger filling her for the first time, but felt his strong arms suddenly pushed her away.

"Bathsheba." His voice returned to its normal controlled tone, as if he remembered his position. "This is not the time or place. The servants could enter at any time. The king has allowed me to take temporary leave from my duties, for this moment, to ensure you are settled in our new home. I am truly glad you are happy to see me. Once we are settled, then maybe we could do ... um ... what you're so hungry for."

Bathsheba raised her hand and backed away.

"You cold, emotionless, son of a dead fish. I almost thought you were human," she said with a smirk as she whirled around and strutted away from him.

"You have the right stature, and you certainly wear the right armor. But, mister, you are missing something. Do you know what would have happened if my handmaids had attempted to enter these chambers unannounced!? They would have quietly closed the curtains and ensured no one else could enter. Why? Because they would have recognized that their mistress and master were finally, *finally* having a quiet, intimate moment. Something they have never observed in the almost six months we've been together."

Uriah swallowed hard. Complexion turned red. Bathsheba's voice was at high pitch now.

"You've come to escort your wife, *your show piece*, to Jerusalem. Fine, then leave so that I may dress the part. Go play soldier for a few more minutes, while I gather my things—as your dutiful wife— and enter the gates of your new assignment."

He stared at his wife for a few moments, then walked toward the tent entrance. He noticed the heavily veiled covering; suggesting that the handmaids had, in fact, observed their presence and was ensuring privacy. Turning, he looked directly at his wife, coughed, and adjusted his armor.

"It's apparent our marriage is not a happy situation for you. I thought you understood I have duties, and the weight of them carry a heavy responsibility. The requirements will also sometimes affect my ability to nurture this relationship. I made a commitment that you will never want for anything. You will always be secure and comfortable. I believe, in time, you will adjust and perhaps we can become better matched."

While Uriah was still talking, Bathsheba moved around the room gathering items, placing them in several satchels. When he paused, she glanced at him. "So, husband, you make a commitment that I will never want for anything. Yes, I'll never want for anything but love, Uriah." She shook her head. "You have no love in you, just fondness and a passion for duty. You and my father make a great match. You should have been the ones to marry."

Uriah picked up his shield, and drew a deep breath. He lifted the tent curtains and was gone. His voice blasted the length of the caravan, shouting orders to his staff to prepare to transfer her entourage to his private escort for the final leg of the trip into Jerusalem. She listened until his voice trailed off, signaling he had moved into the distance.

Bathsheba threw a dress into one of the other bags, then slumped onto the bed and cried. A few short moments later she pushed the cushions away and wiped her face in disgust.

"The military life of a military wife," she mumbled as she continued packing. "Pity party is over."

CHAPTER 5

Bathsheba's personal handmaid, Sasha, came rushing out of the house to grab another package, looking around while walking. "Ma'am, this place is so beautiful."

Bathsheba nodded, smiled, and handed her additional items. "Looking around her new home, she agreed. "I have to admit, these are impressive accommodations."

The two handmaids, who were sent ahead to prepare for her arrival, greeted their mistress with broad smiles of welcome. Bathsheba explored every inch of her new home, designating placement of some of her most favorite paintings, tapestry, sculptures and trinkets. When she entered the bedroom suite, the décor was so well prepared, she was left speechless. The color scheme and design included all of her favorite selections. The blends of lavender, white, and soft pink intricately woven in the fabric, suggested someone was well informed as to what would be pleasing to her eyes.

Clasping hands, Bathsheba laughed. "I don't understand how you all were able to pull this off," she whispered.

"Your mom, ma'am." The handmaid replied. "Your mom directed how your suite should be prepared. The curtains and bedding came from her."

Bathsheba smiled and made a mental note to send a thank you message to her mother, as soon as she had settled for the evening. Opening the doors to the balcony, she threw her cape on the bed.

"Leave the bags in the corner for now. I think I'll relax for a while, before we begin unpacking my things."

As she stepped onto the balcony, her personal handmaid, Sasha, poured a glass of water, placed the tray on the table, then left the room. Bathsheba enjoyed a peaceful leisurely late afternoon stroll on her balcony. The skyline was beautiful in the backdrop of the lush greenery. The well-manicured landscape of flowers that lined the wall overlooking a beautiful garden reminded her of home.

To her right, the city of Jerusalem spread out as far as the eye could see. The white stone houses, many with white crosses on the roof tops, seemed to twinkle from the lamps lit by their occupants in preparation for evening activities. The view brought tears to her eyes and a melancholy tone to her heart.

As Bathsheba continued her stroll, she paused to observe the high stone walls of the palace. It's covering created a space of seclusion and serenity. On this particular side of the balcony, no one could see her—no one could invade her space uninvited. She could escape and enjoy quiet moments, even if Uriah was home. She smiled at the thought of her suite of rooms becoming more like a refuge from the world.

Early evening, Sasha knocked and entered the room with a tray of broth, fish, sweet bread, fruit and a pitcher of water. Her other handmaid, Emerald, followed with more satchels for unpacking.

"Did you have a good rest, ma'am?" Sasha asked while adjusting the bed covers in preparation for her mistress, should she decide to retire.

Bathsheba shrugged and smiled. She searched the tray, selecting the sweet dates, her favorite fruit. "It was alright. All I could hear was activity of people bustling about in the outer courts of the palace below." She laughed while pointing to one corner of the balcony.

"Take a look. Only my husband would ensure we have a home as close as he could get to the king. Only one of the king's 'mighty men' could accomplish such a feat."

Chuckling at the thought, Bathsheba returned to directing the unpacking, when she noticed Sasha was leaning over the balcony waving as if her arms had become disconnected from the rest of her body. "It's King David, ma'am," she shouted.

Emerald ran to the balcony. Bathsheba jumped, then quickly regained her composure.

Walking to the balcony's edge, she admonished her handmaids, "Get a hold of yourself this instant."

Bathsheba had reached the position near Sasha and looked down into the crowd. The sight of King David nearly took her breath away. A black and white gold trimmed chariot pulled him along the path. The king of Israel. He was more handsome than she could ever have imagined. She had goosebumps just looking at him.

Regaining her composure, Bathsheba pushed back from the balcony's edge, fearing that the king might look up and see her.

"Back to the room," Bathsheba said abruptly, and changed the subject. "Let's start by unpacking the large cases. I need my dresses hung immediately."

Emerald moved away quickly. Sasha, stood for a moment quietly observing her mistress, half smiling, but very respectful. "Yes ma'am, of course."

Bathsheba didn't acknowledge the way Sasha looked. Her brief attention to the king or the king's palace was not up for discussion, and canvassed the room, identifying what she wanted done next. She stilled for a moment, lest her actions seemed those of someone embarrassed at being caught red-handed doing something wrong.

To break the silence and the tenseness clearly lingering in the air, in the middle of one of her instructions, she said, "yes, of course, the king is strikingly handsome." She smiled and everyone laughed. Bathsheba issued more orders, while distancing herself even further away from the balcony's entrance.

"Well, let's get as many of my things unpacked as possible, shall we? I understand there are some festivities my husband has planned for me to attend with him later this evening."

She pulled several sheath dresses from her satchel. "I think he leaves for the next campaign in the morning. It's important to him that I am properly introduced to all the right people before he leaves. I need to be ready."

CHAPTER 6

Bathsheba's assumption was well founded. Uriah left for yet another long military campaign the very next morning of their arrival to Jerusalem. It was a welcomed relief.

Night after night, for several weeks, she would go out on her balcony to enjoy the view. Periodically, she even greeted and entertained her grandfather, Ahithophel, in her special space. He had stopped by for a short visit, which was convenient, since he was one of King David's Chief Advisors, and could be called to meet with him at any time. She would listen to her grandfather's stories about recent gallant battles led by the king. The more he talked, the more curious she became about this man called David.

During the day, while watching the handmaids complete their chores, she would listen to the gossip about the house of David.

"Girl, I hear King David is a very unhappy man," Emerald offered while dusting the dining room table. She chuckled. "Imagine, unhappy. In spite of the fact this man has more wives than he has battalions, she laughed."

Sasha chimed in the discussion. "I hear most of the women he married were part of an arrangement or out of convenience, like his first wife Michal, daughter of King Saul. Seems she somehow managed to anger King David to the point he limits her visits to his quarters. Emerald nodded. "Yeah he almost banished her, and after she saved his life too."

"What do you mean?" Bathsheba asked before thinking. She did not mean to encourage gossip.

Sasha, shot her mistress a look of pure astonishment. Emerald answered. "Well, I heard her father, King Saul, sent messengers to kill King David a while back." Emerald stopped cleaning and waved her arm. "Girl, I mean ma'am. It was a mess. I bet now she wish she hadn't." Emerald laughed. "Yep, she saved him several times, at least that's how the story goes."

Sasha nodded. "Well, you know she never had any children. They say that's because God got angry. Rumor is she criticized the King when he danced out of his clothes, happy the Ark of the Covenant was delivered to Jerusalem."

Bathsheba listened to all the gossip, while pretending to be disinterested, and bored. All the while, her interest in King David was peaked. Not wanting it to become too obvious, she ended the discussion. "Ladies, I am ready for some refreshments and a swim. Please prepare a quick meal and bring it to the pool area. I will be there as soon as I've changed."

Sasha and Emerald, recognizing their mistress wanted to be alone, bowed and left Bathsheba to her thoughts.

* * *

Bathsheba spent long, uneventful days in her new home. In an attempt to create a life, she visited several other wives in the area, but found little in common. Most were much older and settled in their daily routine. Everyone had children.

One evening, she entered and scanned the dining area. The meal of lamb roasted in garlic and leaks, and a large platter of melons, figs and sweet bread were prepared, ready and waiting. The table could easily seat twelve people. On this night, as every other night, however, there was only one place setting—hers. Pushing the chair aside, she called Emerald. She had no interest in eating alone again in that large space, representing how empty her life had become.

"Emerald, get Sasha and both of you come here." Emerald bowed and left. Bathsheba gathered the utensils, and napkins. Sasha and Emerald reappeared.

"Grab my goblet and plate. In fact, bring everything. I will be eating on my balcony."

Sasha and Emerald sat with her many evenings during dinner hour, sharing many more insights and gossip about the king and life in the palace. Before long, between the information the maids gathered from visits to the city markets and neighbors, and some associations they developed with people in the palace, she knew a great deal about the life of King David.

One evening after dinner Bathsheba sat in a secluded spot on her balcony. After studying the balcony area, she launched her idea. "Sasha, I want my bath tub to be brought outside here, and I want it prepared as a mini spa, for my use, as soon as possible. Next, I want this entire area accented with white candles."

Bathsheba had ordered all her favorite fragrances and salts be added and that a shear bath screen be situated in front of the tub for additional privacy. When the task was complete, the balcony was transformed. "Ma'am," Emerald offered while placing several towels on the chair near the tub, "your bath is ready."

Bathsheba disrobed and stepped into the warm water. Enjoying the warm air and peaceful atmosphere, she sponged her body while conversing with Sasha and Emerald about the activities planned for the next day. She had finally created her own private paradise.

When finished bathing, Sasha dried, then wrapped her mistress with the large shawl. Bathsheba sat quiet, as the handmaid attended her long hair, patting it with a towel. Emerald prepared her bed.

Maids gone, Bathsheba was alone with her thoughts. The moonlight created shadows on the wall of the room, reminding her of childhood, when she pretended the shadows were playmates. Outside, sounds of soft music and several voices singing a beautiful melody. Turning her face to the wall, pressing deep into the pillow, Bathsheba cried. "I must be tired, she mumbled." In the darkness, with the music still playing, she drifted to sleep.

Meanwhile in the palace, little did Bathsheba know, during her entire bathing ritual, King David was watching. While taking a walk on his balcony, he heard the sounds of laughter that echoed below. Curious, the King leaned over and noticed a breathtaking beauty bathing, attended by two women handmaidens. While enjoying the view his manservant, Lemuel, entered the balcony carrying papers.

"Sire, I need your signature as soon as possible. The messenger awaits."

David ignored his servant's request and waved for him to come to the balcony's edge, pointing to the area where Bathsheba was bathing. "Look there, Lemuel. Who is that?"

Lemuel leaned over the balcony, then turned to King David. "Sire, that is Bathsheba, Uriah's wife." David squinted. "Bathsheba," the King exclaimed. "Couldn't be. She was a little girl last time I remember. That's Bathsheba?!" Lemuel nodded.

King David backed away from the balcony. Silent, while rubbing his beard. "Oh, I see. I knew that was Uriah's house, of course." He chuckled, then cleared his throat. "I thought, however, perhaps his wife had a sister or cousin who might be visiting. But that's his wife you say."

Lemuel half smiled when responding. "Yes, Sire. She is Uriah's wife. The only other females in the house, that I am aware of, would be the handmaids she brought with her."

King David scratched his head, then folded his arms across his chest. "She has grown, this Bathsheba. I vaguely remember the few times she visited with father. She is quite the woman now." Reaching for a pen, he reviewed and signed the papers then dismissed his servant.

The King returned to look over the balcony. It was quiet below, and Bathsheba was gone. David paced the balcony thinking about his first view of Uriah's wife—the granddaughter of his Chief Counsellor, who had become a beautiful woman. He did not want this first look to be the last.

CHAPTER 7

King David paced the floor, while dictating status of new ordinances, before retiring for the evening. He had a full day of hearing and resolving issues brought before him by the people, greeting dignitaries, and reviewing strategic plans for several military operations. One of his attendants was taking notes. The King threw several plans, requiring his review, on the table before crossing the floor to his balcony entrance.

Lemuel, the king's messenger and personal confident, watched his king.

David hit the side of the door with the palm of his hand. "I'm tired. I need a break. I know they're waiting for me to join them on the battlefield, but send word that the rest of the battalion should move forward immediately with one of my chief officers. Let them know I'll join them later, as I need to address several other issues here."

Lemuel gathered the papers, that had been scattered on the table, and put them in a neat pile. "Sire, if you would sign a few of these orders, I will hand them over to the dispatcher, so they are delivered for your leaders to follow."

David nodded and walked over to the balcony entrance. "Bring them to me."

He signed the paperwork then returned to the balcony entrance. He waved his attendant toward the door. "Leave me now, Lemuel. I need some time alone to rest. Make it known I am not to be disturbed."

Lemuel acknowledged the orders, bowed and left. David wandered onto his balcony. He looked to see if the beautiful woman was bathing again. She was not. Instead, Bathsheba was on the terrace enjoying a meal. The king observed the movements of this woman, who had been identified as Uriah's wife.

After the third day observing, when the beauty had disappeared behind the curtains of her room, King David called to his attendant. Lemuel, entered and stood in front of the king's desk awaiting instructions.

King David sat quietly in his chair for several moments, rubbing his chin, then cleared his throat. "I have not been a good king, for I have not taken the time to welcome Uriah's bride to Jerusalem, and apologize for keeping him away from her these past few months."

The King walked to the balcony entrance and stared into the open space. "Go to the home of Uriah and invite his bride to come this evening that I may properly greet her. Go at once."

Lemuel stepped forward. "Shall I order a platter of fish, fruit, vegetables and sweet bread and wine be delivered to your suite, Sire?"

David snapped a sharp, intense look at his messenger servant and friend, then softened and smiled. "Yes, that would be fine."

Lemuel bowed, slowly glanced upward to catch his king's attention with a disapproving glint in his dark brown eyes, then turned quickly, grabbed the handle, and closed the door.

CHAPTER 8

Bathsheba, dry, powdered and draped in a sheer sleeping gown, sat in a cushioned lounge chair inside the bedroom just beyond the balcony doors enjoying the breeze. Her handmaid, Sasha, knocked and opened the door. "Ma'am.," she whispered. You have a visitor with a message."

Wide eyed, Bathsheba arose from her chair and grabbed her sandals. "A visitor," she repeated, while tying her hair back with a scarf. "Get my robe. I wonder who could be calling at this hour?"

Sasha lowered her eyes and shifted, uncomfortable, from one foot to the other. "Yes, ma'am. From the palace. A messenger."

Bathsheba entered the guest area and was greeted by a young man who bowed immediately. "I bring you greetings from King David, with a request that you join him for refreshments now being served."

Bathsheba took one step back to gain composure. "The King, Now?!" She scanned the room. Her eyes settled on the door behind the messenger —the only exit—and inhaled.

"I'm not dressed proper. I will need a moment to prepare."

The messenger bowed again. "Yes, ma'am. I will wait, of course."

The cobblestone streets were quiet and dark, lighted only by the periodic torch lamps from one or two buildings. Bathsheba followed in the footsteps of the messenger, sent to bring her to King David. Turning for a brief moment, she could see her handmaid slowly closing the door to her home, as she maneuvered around the curve of a narrow walkway.

Bathsheba was off balance at every step and needed assistance, twice, to secure her footing. The messenger used a lamp to help guide their journey through the darkness. Other than directing her in specific turns, he was courteous, but quiet.

When they reach their destination, the messenger led her up a set of long, winding marble stairs. On the landing, where several massive doors with wide gold handles covered by the design of a lion's head greeted them. One of the doors opened. Standing before her was that strikingly handsome man she had seen from her balcony the first day she arrived.

King David stepped forward, dismissed the messenger with a nod, and held his hands toward Bathsheba. "Welcome to my home. Please come in."

Bathsheba hesitated, then took his hand while looking around, as if someone was watching. "Thank you Sire," she responded, and followed into a large open room with beautiful hardwood floors, made from cypress, that glistened under the lamps that lined the walls. In the center of the room was a long table with tall candles, on brass holders, surrounded by several platters of figs, grapes, olives, fresh vegetables, bread, and fish.

The King escorted Bathsheba to the table, gestured for her to be seated, then settled onto the large high back chair, at the head of the table.

After a minimal attempt at small talk, the King asked questions to explore her background—much of which he seemed to already know.

As Bathsheba spoke, David sipped wine while studying her face. She paused and eyed him demurely. Placing the goblet on the table, he leaned forward smiling.

"So, I can vaguely remember your father bringing you to the palace when you were quite young. Clearly you have grown gracefully." David gave her an appraising side glance as he poured more wine. "Now, tell me. What has Bathsheba's life been like since her last visit to Jerusalem." He smiled. "Why has it been so many years since I've seen you?"

Bathsheba was so in awe of the king, that she stammered as she began the summary narrative of her life as a military kid. She chose her words carefully, being cautious not suggest any difficult or unhappy times. She didn't want any negative comments to get back to her father.

"Actually, it wasn't too bad growing up. I lived a very typical life, as a military kid. Different schools, sometimes study at home. Lots of beautiful places to visit."

Bathsheba leaned on her elbows. "When I think about it, not many kids can claim to have traveled as much as I did, though it was lonely at times. You have to learn how to adjust to leaving friends, because you're moving to new locations, where you have to make friends over and over again. And, if you're an only child..."

Bathsheba let her voice fade, and sipped the wine. "Other than that, I have few complaints, Sire."

* * *

Bathsheba and the King spent that first evening enjoying each other's company. King David took her on a short tour of the palace, including the beautiful, well-kept gardens. At one point of their walk along the path of white lilies, the king plucked a flower and planted it behind her ear.

"There, now I have two beautiful things to enjoy for the rest of the evening."

Bathsheba was overwhelmed by the attention, the subtle touching, and the way the king thought enough of her to share who he was as a man. She left the palace very early in the morning, while the sun was trying to make its way into the sky.

* * *

Weeks later, after one of her many trips to the palace, Bathsheba entered her home and secured the door. As she walked to her rooms, she was startled by a knock at the door. A familiar voice called her name. She peeped through the door portal, and saw a familiar figure on the pathway, Shabel, her ex-fiancé. He called her name again. Bathsheba paused, looked around to ensure the servants weren't in the area, then opened the door.

Shabel smiled and stepped inside. He Stumbled and wobbled, before gaining balance.

Bathsheba closed the door. "Shabel, what a surprise. What are you doing here?"

Shabel smiled and grabbed Bathsheba, drawing her close. The scent of stale beer or wine nearly knocked her for a loop. He whispered close to her ear, "I've been here for several weeks on family business."

She struggled. "Stop it, what are you doing. I'm married."

Shabel gave low laugh, as his eyes caressed her body. "Yea, I hear you, babe. And so is the King."

Bathsheba froze for a moment, then pushed him away. "What do you mean? What an awful thing to say."

Shabel tossed his head laughing. "You're good. Rumor has it you're the king's new favorite. I just thought maybe you and me could finally get together, since your unexpected marriage prevented the opportunity."

Bathsheba regained her composure, smiled, put both hands on her hips and strutted up to her unwelcomed visitor, while keeping her eyes steadily on his. She leaned so close, their noses almost touch.

"I tell you what Shabel. Why don't I have my maid servant go to the palace with a message from me that I have been attacked by you."

Noticing his discomfort, Bathsheba sauntered back to the doorway, crossed her arms, and leaned on the frame.

"Get this straight, as Uriah's wife and the granddaughter of the King's chief counsellor, I have privileges in the palace. Those privileges include putting anyone who taunts or threatens, or just plain makes me mad in a position that could lead to time in prison, if not death. So, you see, I don't know or care what you've heard. Is that clear?"

Shabel's cocky demeanor diffused, he apologized profusely claiming he may have had too much wine during the evening.

"I hope you can forgive my intrusion and vulgar behavior, Bathsheba" he said as he hurriedly sought to exit the building. At the door, he turned with a pleading look.

"If you could just forget my visit and remember only the good times we had, my love, I would be indebted to you for life."

Bathsheba chuckled. She grabbed the handle of the door and opened wide.

"That's true Shabel. From this day forward, you will be indebted to me for your life. Now leave. Get out of my sight."

Bathsheba was relieved she was able to handle the situation. She didn't want anything to affect the king. She would protect him at any cost. Bathsheba went to bed comfortable in the fact that she had diffused the situation. Gossip is gossip. Nothing could be done about it and she would not let it spoil her relationship with King David.

* * *

For the next few weeks, Bathsheba and King David spent hours together at the palace, or enjoying picnics, and short excursions to other provinces such as Athens, Alexandria, and Damascus. She ignored the whispers and even comments of concern from her personal attendant, Sasha.

"Who am I to deny the king company and conversation?"

Even her grandfather's subtle comments of warning and disapproval served no purpose. She belonged to the king.

The touching and caresses became more intense each evening she visited, until one night the kisses lingered. The expression of love they had for one another evolved into a passionate moment which became the signature covenant of their relationship. This began many more nights they would secretly meet and make love. The king, however, would soon learn there are no secrets in the palace, and every sin has its price.

* * *

Lemuel observed the many disturbing visits of Uriah's wife to the palace. He also spent many days correcting servants, when he happened upon conversations about the couple. His last uncomfortable encounter was walking in on the conversation between King David and his first wife Michal, as she accused him of the infidelity and recounted to him, in detail, her disgust over the many secret encounters he had spent with Bathsheba, that weren't so secret.

After one incident of shouting and accusations, Lemuel was commanded to escort Michal from the King's suite and prohibit her entry to his private areas of the palace until the command changed. For a wife of the king to be banned from his suite was very serious.

One evening, after returning from a long trip, King David was awaiting the arrival of Bathsheba. He commanded the room be prepared in festive lighting and décor. He had been gone a long time and wanted to surprise Bathsheba with a special dinner and gifts he brought with him from his journey. Lemuel knocked and entered the suite.

"Come in," David announced as he looked beyond Lemuel to welcome Bathsheba. "What. No Bathsheba? Is she still dressing?"

Lemuel paused before answering. "No Sire. Actually, I was interrupted when I started toward her home. You have several important dispatches that need your immediate attention and a line of several messengers waiting. I thought you might want to know."

David kicked one of his cushions, then sat at his desk and picked up a pen.

"Very well. Have several handmaids select and prepare a beautiful bouquet of flowers from the garden and send them, with this sealed note, to Bathsheba."

David paced the floor. He had many surprise gifts, gathered during his trip through the region, and had made plans to give them to Bathsheba, one at a time, during their evening together. Now it must wait.

Lemuel completed the instructions and returned to King David's chambers. "The messenger has been sent, Sire."

"Very well then," the king responded, while glancing toward the balcony. "No point in wasting this food. Sit. Eat with me, while I review these important dispatches." He kicked his chair.

Lemuel approached the table, pulled a chair for the king, but didn't sit. He had the unfortunate responsibility of telling the king about rumors that Bathsheba was pregnant. This pregnancy was definitely unfortunate, since the woman's husband had been away too long for the baby to be his.

One of Bathsheba's handmaids was a little too talkative with several handmaids in the palace, and bad news traveled fast—especially through the servant grapevine.

The king glanced, smiled, and waved to Lemuel. "Come. Let's eat before the food is cold." The king pointed to a chair and grabbed a knife to carve the roasted lamb. "Sit."

Lemuel sat, placed his hands of the table, and watched the king carve the lamb in silence.

David stopped carving the meat, dropped the knife on the table, leaned on one elbow, and eyed his servant. "What is it? Speak, as I have much to dictate, and many dispatches for the battalion chiefs."

Lemuel smoothed the leather trim of his arm chair, and cleared his throat. "Sire, I need to share some news with you. There have been discussions throughout the palace that the woman Bathsheba is acting strange and has been sick. Sire, it is rumored she is pregnant."

The king was biting a fig, pulled from the fruit platter, when Lemuel announced the news. He stopped, placed the half-eaten fruit on the plate, folded his dinner cloth, and pushed away from the table. "Indeed. So, the gossip vine is alive and well."

David massaged his beard for a few seconds, then turned to Lemuel. "I need you to bring Bathsheba to me. Do not send a messenger. I need you to go and bring her here."

Lemuel arose from his chair, bowed, and rushed away.

David gripped the edge of the dining table so hard; his hand was bruised from the contact.

CHAPTER 9

Bathsheba rushed to the balcony, when the uproar and cheering crowds became so loud it was difficult to focus on the instructions, she was giving Sasha. She caught a glimpse of King David at a distance before he disappeared into the palace. She had been expecting him for days, so to know he was finally home lifted her spirits. She was eager to be in his presence. She also wanted to confide the news of the child she carried. Bathsheba was so in love, but she was also fearful of what her news would mean. This baby belonged to King David, not Uriah.

Adultery was a violation of the marriage covenant. The penalty was stoning. And she would be the one to catch that end of the punishment, not him.

Bathsheba wanted to look her best this evening and planned to wear her most attractive dress. While deciding which accessories best suited the clothing selection, her handmaid, Sasha entered the room.

"Ma'am, a messenger delivered this note."

Bathsheba smiled, relaxed in her lounge chair, and read the message.

Sasha gathered and hung several of Bathsheba's dresses back in the closet, while waiting. She watched as her mistress folded the message, and laid it on the bed.

Bathsheba turned to Sasha. "I won't be going to the palace tonight. The king has some important dignitaries, with issues that need to be addressed. Just hang the rest of my clothes back in the closet." It wasn't a message she wanted to receive from her love, but felt special it was arrived with beautiful flowers and a special handwritten note.

"Sasha, I'd like some broth and perhaps fruit. I feel like a snack." Sasha smiled, bowed, and left the room.

Bathsheba put the flowers in a vase and picked up the note to read again, when another handmaid knocked and entered the room.

"There is a messenger here from the palace, ma'am. The King wishes to see you now."

Bathsheba paused as she contemplated what she just heard that contradicted the message in her hands. She studied her handmaid as if there was something more for her to say. In the silence, Bathsheba dressed, started for the door, then stopped. She was not ready to see David. She would wait another night. Bathsheba went to her desk and wrote a note.

Turning to the handmaid, "Give this to the messenger, with my apologies to the king. I won't be able to visit tonight." The handmaid took the note and left.

Lemuel returned to the castle, knocked, and entered the king's quarters. King David was seated at the table looking toward the balcony.

"Sire," Lemuel said, while bowing. The woman Bathsheba could not come, but sent this note."

David grabbed the message, read, then folded the paper, and paced the floor some minutes before speaking. "Go again to the house of Uriah. Tell Bathsheba I received the note. She is to come to me this night. It is a command."

Lemuel arose, bowed, and left to complete his mission. A command to report to the king is a call to action that everyone is expected to answer.

King David walked toward the balcony, while reading Bathsheba's note a second time. "My beloved David, I am with child. I have brought shame to you. I love you and I am sorry."

David crushed the paper, threw it in the fireplace and paced the floor.

* * *

King David was seated on one of the large leather cushion chairs, facing the balcony entrance. When Bathsheba entered, he arose and stepped forward; arms open wide. They hugged in silence, then he kissed her long and hard.

"Walk with me," he whispered, as they moved toward the balcony. As soon as she crossed the threshold, Bathsheba faced the man she loved.

"David, you must hate me." She began to cry. "I have complicated our lives. This is such a mess."

King David, placed his finger on Bathsheba's lips, while hugging her tight.

"My love, it is we that have the problem, and we will work it out."

Bathsheba's legs gave way. She dropped toward the floor, still crying. "I love you so much, David. This should be happy news for us both. Instead, I am now an embarrassment to you. Worse yet, I have broken a law that means I lose my life and the life of my baby."

The king gathered Bathsheba in his arms, and carried her to the veranda. They sat for a long while in silence, as she lay on his shoulder sobbing. Only when her crying had subsided, did he share his thoughts.

"I have a plan, my love. I have been contemplating a way to resolve this issue since I heard the news. I will command Uriah to return home. During his stay, you must be intimate with him, so that he believes this child is his."

Bathsheba was shocked at this plan, and disappointed that her love would suggest she perform such an act with her husband when she clearly loved the king. She pushed him away and jumped to her feet.

"You want me to seduce my husband!? You want me to throw my body at him like some whore!" she screamed, then covered her face. "David, how could you ask this of me? What do you think of me? Am I not your true love?" She shook her head. "I won't do it. Not for you and not for my baby."

David grabbed Bathsheba, hugged her firmly, then gave her a long tender kiss. All the while she was crying and pushing him away. He refused to move. He held her until she was quiet and calm again. While stroking the side of her cheek, he whispered, "I know how you feel, my love. I would not ask you to consider doing such a thing if there was some other way. I am the king and must adhere to the laws. I will not lose you." Stroking her arms, David led her to one of the chairs, and kneeled.

"Bathsheba, you are my life. We must work together to hide your condition so you are protected. Please perform this task for me, so that we can be together, or until I find some other way to make peace with the situation."

Bathsheba, still sobbing, nodded.

With details of the plan in place, King David's confidant and messenger, Lemuel, escorted Bathsheba back to her home. No visits the palace would be allowed until after the birth of the baby, a reality that was even more unbearable, given Bathsheba was in the early stages of pregnancy.

Using the night dispatch, King David summoned Uriah to return to

Jerusalem at once. David was confident Uriah would hasten his arrival, because his orders came directly from his king.

* * *

Several days later, Uriah arrived with selected members of his battalion. As they approached his home, the chariot guide slowed to a stop. With full armor, he jumped from the chariot. "Wait here," he commanded. "I will only be a few minutes."

Bathsheba was lounging in her usual favorite spot on the balcony when her handmaid, Sasha, rushed in the room.

"Ma'am, he's here. Your husband is here."

Bathsheba sat up, body rigid. She knew Uriah would be coming eventually, but had hoped she'd have more warning. She repositioned the pillows on the lounge chair and rushed to the bathroom to check her face and hair. "Get some refreshments Sasha. Hurry." Sasha bowed and left.

Uriah was shouting orders and challenging staff on some issue that displeased him. Walking in Bathsheba's room, Uriah shouted, "get those items moved immediately. I'll update on other issues when I return from my meeting." He turned, face Bathsheba, and bowed. Every part of his outfit was positioned and in place, armor shining— he was the perfect soldier boy. "Greetings Bathsheba."

He approached. She stepped back.

Turning toward the balcony, Bathsheba massaged her hands. "So, you're home. How long will I be graced with your visit this time?"

Uriah returned to the bedroom door. "Bathsheba, I have a meeting with the king. Whatever he needs will take priority over any plans I might have. We are in a heated controversy in the region, so my time here is limited."

Bathsheba laughed, "that's been the sum of our married life hasn't it, but I'll order a nice meal for you, Uriah. I will be here when you return."

Uriah's brow furrowed, as his mouth turned grim. "You've kept your bargain well, my wife. The house is well kept and, other than some minor issues, generally running smooth. You understand, of course, I have my duties. I will see you again as soon as appropriate."

Uriah bowed and walked out the open the door just in time for Sasha to enter with the platter of fruit and bowl of broth. Before Bathsheba could ask him to stay for refreshments, he was gone. Sasha, looked at the tray of fruit and broth. Feeling sick, she pushed it aside.

"Take it away Sasha. Share with the servants. I'm tired, I need a nap." Sasha bowed, and removed the tray.

Uriah mounted his chariot. "Move on." He directed the driver to the area beyond the palace.

"We'll settle in the quarters with the rest of the men. Move quickly, I have an urgent appointment with the king."

Uriah visited the soldier's quarters long enough to remove his armor. Eager for an audience with the king, he wasted no time changing attire. A palace man servant escorted Uriah to the king.

When Uriah entered the room, the king was finalizing orders that would be given to Uriah to review in preparation for the next battle. There wasn't anything unusual in the orders—nothing that would require someone of Uriah's position to travel to Jerusalem to see the king. Handing Uriah, the paperwork, King David pointed to a chair nearby.

"Here, sit with me. You have had a long day traveling."

David reached for the flask of wine. "While we eat, tell me first- hand, how the battle is going."

The table was full of a variety of meats, fish, fruit, cheese, lentils and warm broth.

"Eat," King David said, as Lemuel poured a full goblet of wine. Uriah talked as he filled his plate. He felt at home in the king's residence, having been there many times with Eliam. Uriah described, in detail, the various battles won, in spite of many fatalities.

"You would be proud of the men, Sire. They served you well."

Uriah drank much wine that evening, full of high energy and animation when describing every detail of their struggles over and over. He stayed with the king until late day turned late evening. Wine and more wine were poured. Uriah was relaxed and congenial in the atmosphere. He felt privileged that he was able to spend so much time with a person he admired.

As the hour grew late, the king apologized and encouraged Uriah to leave. "Go spend time with your family, Uriah, for I'll need you to meet with me again tomorrow to review the dispatches you'll need to take with you."

Uriah was so impressed with this charge, that he stood at attention, saluted and affirmed his loyalty. "Sire, be assured. You can depend on me."

He then bowed again, not as crisp as usual, but nevertheless suitable. At the door, he turned and smiled. "Thank you for the dinner, Sire. I'll be available as early as you like tomorrow."

The King raised his hand toward Uriah. "Time with your family Uriah. Spend time with your family. I will send a messenger for you something during the day. Now go."

David lowered his head, and studied the floor. The night was long, and thoughts of his beloved being touched by another man was not pleasing.

The plan must be completed. Uriah had to perform his husbandly duties, so Bathsheba would be safe.

He stepped into the warm night, walked over to peer at the home of Uriah. There he saw the light from a candle lamp in the room, just beyond the balcony—Bathsheba's room. He turned away from the scene. The thought of what was taking place almost angered him.

"Good evening Sire."

A voice caught King David off guard. Out of habit, David reached for his sword, always around his waist in battle, but hanging on the wall now. Straining his eyes at the shadow, he recognized the figure standing in the doorway of his suite.

"Ahithophel! What a surprise. Come in," the king shouted as he crossed the floor of the balcony to greet him.

Bathsheba's grandfather bowed to the king, then raised his eyes in the direction of the balcony edge before returning his attention to The King.

David reached for the wine flask and two cups. "Come, sit with me at the table. Have some wine and fruit. Though I'm pleased, you've surprised me at this hour."

Ahithophel took a place at the table, but did not pour the wine. "Sire, I need to speak to you."

David smiled and nodded as he poured wine, grabbed several figs then sat at the head of the table.

Ahithophel had spent many years with the king and understood, unless it was an informal meeting, whenever he takes the chair at the head of the table it was to remind anyone about to speak that he was the king.

"I have a concern about rumors I have been hearing about my granddaughter visiting the walls of the palace regularly in her husband's absence. I don't know who she is seeing, but need your intercession so that these visits cease immediately. It is creating a poor reputation for her."

David sipped the wine slow, while studying his chief counsellor and friend. Setting the goblet down, David leaned forward and clasped his hands on the table.

"Ahithophel, I assure you this night your concerns will be investigated. Whatever has been discussed, must be grounded in baseless gossip. If your granddaughter has visited the palace, there is a logical explanation. Whatever the situation, I will see that it is rectified."

"Thank you Sire. I am sure you understand I value my family and its reputation. We've had good years here."

Ahithophel stood, bowed and raised his eyes to look directly at the face of his king.

"It's a good night for sleeping, Sire. I pray you have a restful one." King David smiled, but did not respond. He watched his old friend leave, then returned to pace the balcony that night until early morning.

* * *

Just before dawn, Lemuel opened the door to his king's quarters, and found him sleeping in a cushion chair near the balcony. "Sire," he whispered.

King David stirred, but didn't open his eyes. Lemuel leaned closer.

"Sire, I need to speak with you. It is urgent."

David stretched, rubbed his face, and opened his eyes to see the unsmiling face of his messenger servant.

"He did not go home, Sire. Uriah slept with his troops last night. I had him observed. Not once did he visit his home. The lady, Bathsheba, slept alone."

David studied the floor. He was quiet so long that Lemuel took one step back, waiting.

Slamming his hand on the chair arm, David shouted, "What manner of man is this fool? Who comes home after months away from his bride and spends his one and only night in the palace barracks?!

Jumping from the chair, King David paced the length of the suite.

"What the ... Who does this? Bring him to me. Bring him to me now!" Lemuel bowed and left the room.

* * *

Uriah arrived, scored by Lemuel, at the king's bidding. "Sire, I await your instructions."

King David paced back and forth in silence for several moments, then stopped, went to his desk, grabbed a pen and began writing.

"Uriah, I need you to stay here another day. I have several important tasks I need you to attend to, before completing my next set of instructions for the foreign campaign."

After completing the written instructions, King David, threw the pen on the desk, rubbed his hands together, then folded them across his chest. "The legion of troops here at home are slack in their formation, attire, and reporting processes. I need you to spend time today meeting with several of the commanders, and provide an overview of recommendations to me this evening. I realize this is tedious, but it will be helpful," King David said, as he stamped the orders.

Uriah grinned. "Sire, I'd be happy to assist. I will get started immediately."

King David returned the smile, moved away his desk, and approached Uriah. Laying a hand on his shoulder, the King beckoned Lemuel to come forward.

"Take Uriah to the master battalion headquarters on the southside."

David returned his attention to Uriah. "You will dine with me again this evening, and provide a detailed report."

Uriah adjusted is armor, saluted, bowed to the king, and left to complete his assignment.

King David lowered his head briefly, then returned to the desk.

Leaning back in his chair, he looked toward the balcony.

* * *

At the end of the day, David sent for Uriah to again join him for repast and conversation. The King ensured much wine was had, and listened again to the endless ramblings of his young soldier's battle triumphs. Uriah then reported his findings, and recommendations from investigations of the day. Lemuel was on hand to take notes, and ensure wine glasses remained full.

As the hour grew late, King David again apologized for keeping Uriah for keeping him away from his home.

"You have done well. Go, spend time with your wife. I will send Lemuel to you in the morning with orders for related to strategies for the campaign we face in the north."

Uriah bowed. "Yes Sire, and thank you for yet another inspirational evening in your presence. As usual, I have learned a great deal."

King David put his arm around Uriah's shoulder, and walked him to the door. "Yes. It was a good evening. Now, enough work. I suggest you relax with family. I will see you in the morning."

King David spent another restless night knowing he sent Uriah home to Bathsheba. Several times, he stood at the balcony entrance, taking deep breaths to try to slow his heartbeat and busy himself with other thoughts. Once, he stepped onto the balcony, and stood still. Looking around, all he could see was darkness. The city was sleep, and he heard nothing but the sound of a dog barking in the distance. With clinched fists and slumped shoulders, he returned to the chambers, dressed and climbed into bed.

* * *

The King awoke early the next morning, but didn't move. He scanned the room. The sun was already streaming through the opening to the balcony. A soft breeze moved the window curtains. He propped his pillows and sat quietly watching the curtains dance. A knock at his door disturbed the silence.

"Enter," he shouted. The door opened with Lemuel stepped in.

David arose, put on his robe, and grabbed his sandals.

"Sire," Lemuel said as he bowed. "I have more news for you." He stepped closer in the room.

"Uriah again slept with his troops in the barracks here in the palace."

David took one of his sandals, and threw it across the floor. "What is it with this idiot? Why did he not do as I commanded?" He shouted.

Lemuel reached for the king's shoe and handed it to him. "Sire, you did not command Uriah to go home, you suggested he get some rest, and mentioned he should spend time with his wife. Uriah is a soldier. He operates on commands. All other comments are suggestions, giving him a choice." Lemuel picked up a flask, poured a cup of water and offered it to the King.

"He did not feel he was disobeying an order, Sire. In his view, you offered recommendations and options. He chose to take the option to spend yet another night with his troops."

The King took the water and sipped. Throwing the cup down, he shouted. "He's a fool. A blind, stupid fool. He will enter the battle this day. He will enter the battle and die. May God forgive me."

Lemuel didn't move. David stopped his ranting, and turned to his servant, speaking in a low tone.

"Lemuel, bring me Uriah."

King David slumped his shoulders, and dropped into his chair. "I told him you would deliver the orders that he is to take with him today. Instead, go. Bring him to me. I will write a new set of orders, and I want to give them to him myself."

Uriah was so excited the king had called for him again, he almost ran, taking the steps two at a time with Lemuel trying to keep pace. Upon reaching the chambers, Uriah knocked and entered immediately, offering a warm greeting.

David responded with a smile that didn't quite reach his eyes. "Uriah, I need to make one adjustment in the dispatch I had planned to give you." David shuffled the papers on his desk and reached for his pen.

"In addition to the way you've handled yourself here, I have been very pleased with the way you led, and won, the last few campaigns. There is another area, however, where I think you would be of better use to me. A fierce battle is taking place to the Southeast of our borders, and I am concerned about how it is being managed. What do you think about supporting their efforts? It would only take you away from your regular duties for no more than a few weeks."

Uriah stepped forward smiling. "Sire, I would be proud to take on this assignment. I shall leave immediately."

"Good. Very good." King David responded, then wrote a special message to the commander of the fiercest battle in that region that outlined specific instructions related to Uriah. It included that Uriah was to be placed in the forefront of the most heated confrontation, with no support as his rear guard. Uriah was not to survive the battle. If necessary, one of King David's own soldiers was to ensure the king's order was fulfilled. When the deed was completed, King David was to be notified.

King David placed the message in an envelope, sealed it with his official ring stamp, and handed the details to Uriah.

"Here, take these instructions. They are to be given to and opened by the chief battalion commander only. Is that understood?"

"Yes Sire." Uriah saluted. "I appreciate the opportunity to serve."

Both Uriah and Lemuel bowed and left. David sat quiet at the head of the table in his high back chair, tapping his fingers on the table.

Uriah left the palace with several of his soldiers at his side. While leaving Jerusalem, his chariot traveled past his home. The chariot attendant paused.

"Sir, do you want me to pull up here for a moment?"

Uriah looked at the house door and started to dismount. He stopped. "No, continue. This will be my first stop on my return."

The chariot attendant proceeded. Uriah smiled, as he turned the corner, on the road away from Jerusalem, to meet his destiny.

COMMENTARY

The story of Bathsheba begins with the view of a young woman whose early life was spent as an only child in a military family. There is no mention of siblings and like so many young girls, she had to develop her own survival techniques to adapt to the challenge of having to make friends over and over again or to just being alone for months with only her mother and father as company.

Considering Bathsheba's grandfather was also military—chief counsellor of King David—one can only imagine the disappointment that she wasn't a "he." In spite of those unfortunate consequences, historical details suggest she may have travel with her father, in her youth, and could easily have visited the palace of King David as a child—long before the ill-fated relationship eventually leading to infidelity.

Bathsheba's marriage to Uriah, though not detailed in the Bible, may have been an unhappy experience, as there were no children and the limited discussion of her husband is focused on his undying dedication, love, and loyalty for King David. He was all military.

King David was the catalyst for the destruction of an entire family unit. Beginning with the adulterous affair and pregnancy of a young family member of both his "mighty men" and chief counsellor, this family was humiliated and brought to social ridicule as a result of passion and lust. David was the King. He was "the man after God's own heart," so all the players in this scenario were in awe of him and offered undying loyalty in spite of the situation. This soon changed for at least one of them, at the death of Uriah, followed by the quick marriage and birth of the King's son, by Bathsheba.

History reveals that Bathsheba's grandfather eventually joined forces with King David's son, Absalom, in an attempt to murder the king, suggesting Ahithophel's hate and disgust for David reached an irreparable state. History also reveals that King David did not go unpunished for the choices he made, but his story also demonstrates how the love of God and his forgiving nature enables us to still do great things for him. David and Bathsheba paid the price of their choices by the loss of their child created in sin, but by grace they were blessed in the birth of a son, Solomon, who became known as the wisest and richest man who ever lived, and part of the lineage to Jesus.

STORY TWO: HOUSEWIFE OF ARAMEAN: REBEKAH AND ISAAC

CHAPTER 10

"The will of God will not take you
where the grace of God will not protect you."
— Bernadette Devlin

Eleazar, Abraham's trusted servant, returned to his home after having sworn an oath to his master that he would go to Nahor to search for a wife for Abraham's son, Isaac.

Standing in the doorway of his modest dwelling, he hesitated. He now had to convey this assignment to his wife. Greeting her with a kiss on the cheek, Eleazar stepped into the kitchen and sat down.

Carmel shot a curious glance, nodded, and continued seasoning the fish with spices and herbs, in preparation for what would be part of a special dinner she was planning. Eleazar's birthday was in several days, and she had invited friends over to celebrate. "Well, you're here early. Your duties for the day are completed already?"

"Yes ... well ... about that." He cleared his throat. "I had to temporarily reassign my duties. I've been given a special assignment that will take me away from here for a while.

"Oh?" She gave him a sideways glance while dusting the ball of dough with flour. "What exactly does he want you to do?"

He heard the unspoken warning. The message was, "I'm in a good mood; don't test me." The way she became overly aggressive in pushing the heel of her hand into the dough only confirmed his suspicion that she wouldn't take this news well. He rubbed his hand across his head before answering. "Master Abraham wants me to depart within the next few days to Nahor."

Carmel stopped working the dough, wiped her hands with the kitchen towel, leaned on the counter, and studied his face. "Nahor is not around the corner, Eleazar. Why in the world does Abraham need you to travel so far? You've never had an assignment like this. You're his lead household servant. He put you in charge of everything here. What could possibly create a need for you to travel such a long distance?"

Eleazar closed his eyes and pinched the bridge of his nose. "Well." He leaned back in his seat. "Master Abraham wants me to find a wife for his son."

Carmel chuckled, walked away from the kitchen counter, and took a chair at the table next to her husband. "You're kidding me, right? Isaac is at least in his late twenties—a grown man. He has a home of his own, and he's very capable of selecting a wife right here. But you have to travel with him to Nahor to help find one? Really? That's ridiculous." She threw the towel on the table and sat back in the chair laughing.

Eleazar was silent for a moment, then got up, grabbed a flask of water and filled a cup. "Actually, Isaac isn't allowed to make this trip." After taking a sip, he brought the flask and cup of water to the table, and sat again. "I have to go alone, loaded with gifts from Master Abraham for the bride-to-be and her family—once I select her, that is."

"First thing, Eleazar," his wife corrected. "You're inside our home, so stop with the 'master' stuff, and let's just call him Abraham, shall we?" She pushed back from the table so hard that she almost made the flask tip over. "So, Isaac can't go to Nahor, but you have to go and select a woman to bring back here to be his wife. If this doesn't beat all the stories I've heard about this family, I don't know what does."

Arms crossed, she paced the floor, her eyes staring fixedly at her husband. "Abraham is the same man who would have slaughtered his son if God hadn't provided a *ram in the bush*, as the story goes."

Carmel shook her head, and let out a ragged sigh. "If he trusts God so much, why doesn't he ask God to direct his son to the woman ordained to be his wife? Or better yet, ask God to send her to Isaac—just drop her in his lap. Why doesn't he pray instead of sending his servant almost a hundred miles away to bring one home," she shouted. "You can't possibly be serious."

Eleazar shifted in his seat and raised his hand for silence. "Enough, Carmel. No matter what his reason is for doing it this way, Abraham has been good to us. He asked me do this, and that's what I'm going to do. I'll leave and return as soon as my assignment is complete.

His wife rolled her eyes then looked away.

"Let's not fight over this, beloved," he coaxed. Rising from his chair, he extended a hand to her. "Help me prepare for my journey."

When she didn't respond or move toward him, he kissed her gently on the cheek and left the room. Carmel sighed, looking at the cupboard where she'd hidden his birthday gift. "Master Abraham indeed," she mumbled, as she returned to the meal preparations.

As he had sworn by solemn oath, Eleazar followed Abraham's instructions without fail. With prayer, diligence, and faith that the angels of the Lord went before him, he entered the country of his master's birth and met, by providence, the woman whom he selected as the bride for Isaac. His next step—and perhaps the most important—would be to ensure her willingness to return with him to Canaan.

CHAPTER 11

"Hey, Sis, I think we can easily call your chance meeting with the old guy at the well a Divine connection."

Rebekah's brother, Laban, chuckled as he casually walked the dirt path, counting the camels loaded with gifts. "Good ole uncle Abraham sure sent a hefty endowment for the woman chosen to marry our cousin, Isaac."

Rebekah rolled her eyes, irritated at her brother's obvious display of greed over the bounty he and his family were about to receive. "That's just like you, brother dear," she sneered. "It's always about profit or getting over, isn't it?" Speeding her pace to catch up with him, she tugged his arm. "If father were still alive, you'd have much to answer for after that comment."

Laban hugged his sister, tickled her chin, then grabbed one of the packages and inspected the contents. "You're probably right. But you can't deny that you just hit a gold mine opportunity with this chance meeting. I'd call this being in the right place at the right time." He smiled and winked. "Anyway, you can't talk about me always thinking about profit."

He gave her a knowing smile. "I didn't see you return that gold nose ring and those arm bracelets the old man gave you at the well."

Rebekah yanked from her brother's hold, stepped back and threw both hands in the air. "You need to stop. You're embarrassing me," she said in a hushed whisper.

She gave a slight nod in the direction of the well a few hundred feet away. Eleazar was leaning against the structure, observing the exchange between the siblings.

"Like I already told you," she said. "This man is a trusted servant messenger who was sent on a mission. He traveled a great distance, on faith, as a representative of his master, who happens to be our uncle. He wasn't sent to visit us. His mission was to find a wife for his master's son."

Rebecca crossed her arms, narrowed her eyes, and looked straight at Laban. "And yes, after he prayed, I arrived at the well with the water jar in answer to his prayer." She whirled around, raised her head and ran toward the house. "Now, I must find mother," she shouted over her shoulders. "Feel free to continue your mission, my greedy brother. All you can do is count the bounty."

Laban shrugged, gathered the package he'd opened and waved to Eleazar. "Come. You're welcome in our home. Follow me." He led the way as Eleazar followed, keeping a few paces behind.

Rebekah entered the house, ran past the entrance to her father's old study and down the hall. A small stone patio lined with lilies and red roses connected the study to the rest of the house. She went up three narrow steps and burst into Milcah's room.

Giving her mother several quick pecks on the cheek while dancing, Rebekah stopped to catch her breath long enough to share her news. "Mother, stop what you're doing right now. Let me tell you what just happened to me."

Milcah held up her hands in a jester of surrender, and laughed.

Rebekah, still moving, ignored her response. "I've been asked to marry uncle Abraham's son, Isaac. Well, kind of. It's just so crazy and complicated, but wonderful."

Rebekah danced around the room again, then stopped directly in front of her mother and held out her arm. "See? Look at the bracelets and nose ring he gave me. It's so exciting. Uncle Abraham must be very rich. That means his son is rich." Rebekah laughed. "I'm going to marry a rich man!"

Milcah set the materials aside, brushed her hands, left her weaving table, and took her daughter's hand. Smoothing Rebekah's hair, she smiled. "Calm down, baby." She patted the chair next to her.

"Come. Sit with me a moment. This is too much and not enough information at the same time. One moment you're doing your daily chore of gathering water, and the next you are making plans to get married. All this before our first meal." She laughed. "Let's take this one step at a time. You're young, so any discussions about your moving away and getting married makes no sense to me right now. Don't let these gifts cloud your vision."

With a big hug, Milcah whispered to her daughter, "you stay here. Relax and settle your mind. Enjoy the warm breeze coming from the garden, and meditate on these recent events. I'll go and listen to what this man has to say."

Her mother walked to the door, then turned to observe Rebekah for a moment. "Remember, you wait here in my room and pray while your brother and I have a discussion with Abraham's servant messenger. Then you and I will talk more about it." Smoothing her hair and adjusting her clothes, Milcah left the room.

Rebekah did as she was told. Sitting still, letting her thoughts revisit the day's events. She smiled, closed her eyes, and prayed.

* * *

Abraham's servant messenger, Eleazar, bowed as Milcah entered the room. At the prompting of Laban, Eleazar proceeded to explain the purpose of his visit to Nahor and repeated the incident at the well. "Ma'am, I'm a trusted servant of Abraham and it's my sincere belief that your daughter, Rebekah, was chosen by God to return with me to marry my master's son, Isaac."

Before his mother could respond, Laban gestured to the window. "Mom, look." He hooked his arm under Milcah's and walked her to the opening. "See there, beyond the gate? There must be at least ten or twelve camels, all laden with gifts for us. Surely Rebekah would be well received in this new life. This is truly a sign from the Lord, and we really have no right to refuse."

Rebekah's mom reviewed the expansive caravan, turned away from the window and studied the old man. Instead of shifting and avoiding eye contact, Eleazar looked directly in her eyes.

"Well." She shrugged. "It's not like this servant represents a stranger. This is family." She looked at her son, and nodded in agreement. "Okay, go get her, Laban. Let's ask Rebekah again, to be sure this is what she wants. She is so young for such a venture, but I don't want her to miss an opportunity to live well and fulfill her destiny."

Laban knocked and quickly entered his sister's room. "Hey, look. Mom and I talked. We agree you would have a promising future if you marry Isaac."

Rebekah stared at her brother for a long while.

He shifted his stance to avoid eye contact. "But, of course, we want you to have the last say. If it's no, it's no." He gazed at her with a broad smile and she could tell he was counting their blessings once again. "Come on, Sis, let's go to the living area where we can all talk." Laban extended his hand toward her.

Rebekah smacked Laban's hand and pushed it away. "Cut it out Laban." With a half laugh, she opened her mother's bedroom door.

"You and I both know your interest is not in my welfare. You saw another opportunity for you to take advantage of a situation. I get it."

Pausing at the door, she faced Laban, her expression pensive. "Just remember that this time, it's all about me. You can fool mom, but you can't fool me. Now, let's go and have a final meeting with the servant messenger who holds the keys to my future."

When Rebekah and Laban arrived to the guest living space, the room was bright and cheerful. Facing the sunny side of the building, rays of the sun hit the sheer curtains and bounced off the furnishings just right. The handmaids were leaving, having prepared bowls of fresh fruit and honey buns for the guest table, with flasks of fresh water on the stand nearby.

Eleazar acknowledged Rebekah and Laban's presence with a bow, then returned his attention to their mother. "I recognize your daughter is young, ma'am, but she was clearly sent to me in answer to the prayer my master laid before the Lord, seeking a wife for his son."

Eleazar reached in one of several packages he had brought inside and unveiled gifts of silver, gold, and clothing. He handed them to Rebekah. He also gave multiple expensive gifts to Laban and her mother.

Fingering all the finery, Laban turned to Rebekah and smiled. "This is truly a gift from God. Rebekah, are you ready to go and become a wife?"

Rebekah raised her eyebrows, cutting a side eye in Laban's direction.

"Well," Laban offered. "That's what you already said, sort of. Didn't you?"

Ignoring her brother's comment, Rebekah smiled at her mother then turned to face Eleazar. "Clearly I'm taking a big chance trusting your word, but from what you described, this is great opportunity to live in very comfortable surroundings."

Eleazar smiled.

Rebekah turned back to her mother and brother. "I believe this servant messenger was sent by God and did pray for His guidance. I believe it was a divine moment. This feels right to me." Reaching for Eleazar's hand, she said, "Yes, I'll go."

Laban laughed aloud and Milcah hugged her daughter. Eleazar spent the rest of the evening sharing stories about life in the land of Abraham, and gave even more gifts to the family.

The next morning while Rebekah was busy packing, Laban and Milcah arranged to meet with Eleazar regarding an addendum to the plan. This new piece of the puzzle was Laban's brainchild.

When Eleazar arrived, Milcah was seated in her cushioned chair by the window, putting last minutes touches on a small tapestry gift she stayed up late to weave as a gift to her daughter. She nodded at their visitor and smiled but didn't speak.

Laban, however, was pacing the living area, inspecting the gifts they had received the evening before.

Eleazar coughed to make his presence known to him.

Fingering one of the golden bracelets, Laban waved for him to be seated. "My mother and I were discussing that perhaps you might let my sister stay home with us an additional ten days to help her become more adjusted to the idea of marriage. You could feel free to leave the packages here and, when you return, she would be more ready for the trip."

Very disturbed at this abrupt change in the agreement, Eleazar raised his hands, while pleading for a change of heart. "Please, master, don't delay this blessing. God is clearly in this plan. I prayed to find the right choice for a wife for my master's son. It was my master's charge that when the choice was made, I should return with her as soon as possible. Last evening, you, your mother"—he bowed to Milcah— "and your sister agreed it was the right decision for her to return with me so she could marry my master's son."

Moving closer to Laban, with hands clasped as if praying, the servant messenger continued. "Sir, we must move forward. Please let us leave."

Laban and Milcah looked at each other, but before any other words could be exchanged, Rebekah entered the room. Neither her brother nor mother offered a greeting. Everyone was looking at her. She scanned their faces.

Rebekah walked to her mother and gently grasped her hand. She could see her eyes were watering. "Mother, what's wrong? I'm packed and ready."

Laban breathed heavily. "So, Sis, mom and I were just saying that maybe you could stay here another ten days to make sure you are comfortable with the idea of getting married."

Rebekah whirled around to face him. Hands squeezed into fists; she took several steps in his direction. "Enough of this Laban. I have no intention of allowing you to work on a plan to milk the situation to your own personal gain. There is no possible reason for me to wait. You and mom agreed last night, and this is what I want to do."

Laban lifted his shoulder in a half shrug, but didn't say another word.

Rebekah hugged her mother firmly. "This is truly what I want to do. It's a glorious adventure and it's not like you haven't heard of Abraham. My goodness, he's grandfather's brother—well established and well respected in his country. I'm sure his son is equal in this regard."

She stepped closer to Eleazar. "Don't forget that this man came here on a mission to ensure that his master's son would have a wife who shares his beliefs and customs, rather than having him marry a woman unsuitable to their faith." Rebekah focused her gaze on her mom. Tears ran down her cheek. "It has to be right, and I believe this is my destiny."

Moving toward the door, she glared at Laban. Rebekah paused, gathered the last of her things, and nodded to the Eleazar.

In the doorway, she cast one final look at her mother and brother. It was softer, more congenial. "Please don't worry."

Looking down, Laban began kicking his feet as if something was stuck to the floor. He never looked up at her again. Her mother smiled through her tears.

Rebekah began the trek to a life in Canaan, with a nurse and three handmaids by her side and hope in her heart.

Back at the house, Milcah remembered the tapestry on her sewing bench. "Oh, my goodness. I forgot to give my baby her farewell gift." She dropped in a chair and cried.

CHAPTER 12

I 'm not suggesting you run in the street and grab a woman." Abraham spoke to his son in a calm voice, trying not to show his impatience. "And definitely not in these streets. But it's time for you to move on with your life and find a wife."

Abraham was standing in the garden his wife, Sarah, had planted and cared for before her death. Isaac had visited this spot twice a day for the last three years. He stayed close to home, barely socializing until one day his father had him move to a town close by, all in hopes of encouraging him to move on with his life. The plan worked to some extent, as now his son visited this site less regularly. Isaac had just finished placing fresh flowers on his mother's grave. Brushing the dust from his hands, Isaac faced his father, agitated. "Why is this becoming a problem between us? I get my work done. I don't understand the issue."

Abraham grabbed his son firmly by the shoulders. "Isaac, I recognize everyone experiences the loss of a loved one in a unique way, but your grieving has not been healthy. You spend too much time here. It's been three years. Your mother is gone. She wants you to live. It's time for you to get married and have a family."

Isaac lowered his head, covered his eyes with his hands and listened to his father's counsel in silence. Abraham smiled, hugged his son, then guided him away from the patch of earth that held his beloved wife. "Let's walk."

Abraham took one last look at the gravesite. The sun had cast a shadow over the stone marking. The air was dry, with a slight breeze blowing the bouquet of flowers they left. He shifted his attention back to Isaac.

"I think your mother and I have done you a disservice by keeping you as close to home as we have all these years. But I'm going to fix that. I promise you. A few days ago, I sent Eleazar to search out a wife for you from my brother's country. He should be returning soon. She'll help you move forward and live."

Isaac studied the aging man he loved so dearly. "Uh, father, you sent a servant all the way to Nahor to find me a wife? Why? There are plenty women right here."

The two men reached the confines of their home on the large family estate. Tired, Abraham sat on the veranda and beckoned his son to join him. Shifting to adjust his back that had experienced much stress through hard work in his youth, Abraham touched his son's shoulder gently.

"I really would prefer if you marry a believer, son," he said. "And the choices here are few and far between. Though I know you have been dating, there's too much uncertainty about their lifestyles, beliefs, and choices. I believe God's choice for you will be found in Nahor. I only ask that you trust me."

Isaac shrugged and slapped both hands on his knees. "Alright, so our trusty servant will find me a wife." He shook his head and smiled at Abraham. "And she will make you a grandfather."

They both hugged and remained in their own thoughts for several minutes, then proceeded into the house for the evening meal.

* * *

The Journey to her new home was long and tiring. They had to stop several times because of Rebekah's discomfort with long stretches of time on the camel. Eleazar was very attentive, ensuring she was refreshed regularly.

They arrived in Canaan at midday. Eleazar slowed the caravan to a halt and pointed. "Ma'am, your future husband is on the road ahead."

Rebekah dismounted the camel and immediately covered her face with a veil. "I must greet this man Isaac. How fitting that we should meet on the road to my new home. This is so exciting." She turned to the servant and said, "Come, introduce me to my new husband."

The pebbles from the road attached to her sandals and in between her toes as she walked two or three steps ahead of Eleazar. Several stones cut some of the skin on her feet, but in her excitement, she barely felt anything. When they reached Isaac, she bowed. Isaac could not see her smile behind the veil, but he was pleased with her beautiful eyes.

Eleazar cleared his throat. "Sir, this is Rebekah, your distant cousin from Nahor."

Rebekah stepped forward and smiled. "I am so happy to meet you. I am to be your wife."

Isaac hesitated to speak at first, but looked in her eyes and smiled. Taking her hand, he inclined his head. "Happy to meet you, cousin Rebekah of Nahor. I just recently returned from my home in Negriv, not far from here. I was heading to my father's home in preparation for your arrival."

Holding his hand firmly, Rebekah laughed. "So now we can journey there together."

Isaac nodded in agreement, but remained silent as they walked the short distance to his father's home.

Rebekah continued leading the conversation. "So, my grandfather is your father's brother. Isn't that something?" Gesturing toward Eleazar "So, I met this older servant of yours at my town well. He told me I was sent in answer to a prayer for someone to marry his master's son. Who would've thought his master's son would be my cousin?" She laughed, stopped, and looked at Isaac with a welcoming smile.

He didn't return that smile. Looking at the ground, smoothing the dirt with his sandals, Isaac shrugged. "It's a shame we had not met before now, but our families are spread so far and wide. I mean, had we known each other, we could have had many moments to talk and get to know one another." He made no other comment.

Rebekah laughed as they started to walk again. "You don't talk much do you, Isaac?"

"Why should I? You're doing enough talking for the both of us." Rebekah side eyed him, and they both laughed.

Arriving at their destination, they were greeted by Abraham with warm hugs. "You two rest today." He turned to Rebekah. "I've had a special room prepared for you. Just have your handmaids follow one of the servants to carry your things."

With an arm around Rebekah, Abraham turned to his son. "Isaac, you know where your room is." He laughed and slapped him on the back. "I've been waiting for this day and have a little surprise for you both."

Directing them to one of several chairs in the room, Abraham said, "Several of our neighborhoods have been notified to be on call to help celebrate your marriage ceremony." Excitement filled his tone. "It won't be a large gathering, but the ceremony is arranged for tomorrow, followed by a dinner feast. We'll have an arch covered with white silk and decorated with red and white roses."

Abraham moved from spot to spot, showcasing where everything would be laid out. "The room will be lined with torch lights in brass holders, accented with red roses and water lilies. The table setting will include special tableware that was a favorite of your mother, Isaac. Our staff worked all day on the details. Abraham waved for one of the staff to come forward. "As for the food, here is Eleazar's wife. She has been my right hand in his absence. Because of her, every combination of fish, lamb, broth, in addition to mixed vegetables, honey buns, nut cake, and more will be available."

Rebekah was so pleased, she was giddy. "Oh, my goodness. This is overwhelming. I so appreciate your efforts." She laughed and kissed her future father-in-law on the cheek. "I don't have a wedding dress, but your servant brought so many beautiful outfits to my home, I'm sure I can find one that will fit the occasion."

Abraham put both hands on Rebekah's shoulders. "My dear, as beautiful as you are, the clothes will only compliment what is already there."

Isaac was quiet through all the greetings and hugs. Clearing his throat before arising from the chair, he walked toward the exit. "Well, I think I'll get cleaned up and settled in."

Rebekah moved away from Abraham and reached for Isaac's hand. "You're so quiet. Is anything wrong? I guess you're overwhelmed too," she laughed.

Isaac hesitated a moment, squeezed her hand, then released it. He turned to his father. "You didn't tell me about all this activity planned for our marriage ceremony. I thought it was to be something simple, quiet. This seems a bit extravagant. Though I grew up here, I've had very little real interaction with the neighbors. Other than the social activities you and mom arranged around your social gatherings; I've kept pretty much to myself. Remember, this was your mandate, including that I not marry anyone in this area.

He rubbed his goatee while looking between his future wife and father. "Look, why don't we reduce the number of guest and keep it small and intimate, reducing the hassle around food prep, and the clean up after the event."

With his statement, the atmosphere changed to one of discomfort and unease. Rebekah found a chair and sat down, watching father and son eye each other as though they were strangers.

Abraham sighed, and reached for his son. "Isaac, this isn't a big celebration. It's an acknowledgement of how happy you have made me. I just wanted to share the moment, in a small way, with neighbors and a few good friends. All you need to do is stand with your beautiful bride and enjoy the best wishes coming your way. I won't ask you to make a speech, and you can escape from the crowd after dinner."

Isaac glanced at Rebekah, who was looking directly at his father. "I don't want to ruin the plans, of course, and I appreciate all you've done, father." Shifting from one foot to the other, Isaac mumbled, "Okay, let's move ahead with the plans. I'll do whatever needs to be done to make it happen."

Rebekah jumped up, laughed and wrapped her arms around Isaac's neck. She kissed him on the cheek and whispered, "Thank you."

Abraham had been a little dishonest when it came to "no fanfare" in planning the ceremony. He sent his servants, the day of their arrival, with invitations for all their neighbors. Everyone in the household, and some servants on loan from the neighbors, worked through the night. For the short notice, it was as an extravagant affair as possible.

The entire house and patio gardens were decorated with every combination of flowers that could be found. White sheer cloth accented with garland and flowers draped the chairs, matching the canopy archway that had been built for the occasion. Rebekah waited, with her handmaid, in one of the side rooms waiting to be escorted to the ceremonies. "Ma'am you look so beautiful. Your mother would be so proud."

Rebekah nodded then glanced sideways. She didn't want the servant to see her tears. She missed her mother. Changing the subject, she pointed to the material on the cushioned chair. "Let's get my veil, shall we. I want to be ready to go as soon as they call."

Moments after her face was covered with the veil, two quick knocks and the door opened. Several maid servants rushed in to announce the groom awaits.

Abraham stood in the doorway smiling, arms outstretched. "Come, let us go make you, officially, my daughter."

Rachel smiled, hugged her father-in-law to be, and took his arm. "I look forward to becoming Isaac's wife and your daughter."

After a brief ceremony, as promised Isaac, the celebration began. Lots of food, music, laughter, and dancing permeated the atmosphere. It was a jovial exchange between neighbors sincerely happy to see Abraham smiling again. Everyone enjoyed the activities. Everyone, that is, except Isaac. At one point, he was so overwhelmed with the crowds and chatter, he ceremonially whisked his bride out of the area as soon as it was decently possible.

Rebekah, mildly agitated at having to leave her wedding celebration so early, turned abruptly to him as he closed the door to their room. "I don't understand, Isaac. We just left a wonderful celebration in our honor that your father went to great lengths to prepare. Most of the time, you looked like you were bored and disinterested and you barely spoke to our guests. What is it with you and this distant behavior?"

Isaac reached out and wrapped her securely in his arms. "My focus is you. No one else. For years, the activity in this house was my mother, my father and me. Though my parents traveled around visiting with neighbors and friends, or attending meetings, there was very little activity here. Because of my father's leadership role, my mother ensured our home was more of a sanctuary—away from crowds. If we had any group meetings here, my mother managed all the activity so that people understood their limitations. It's how I grew up. It's who I am."

He lifted Rebekah's hand and kissed her fingers. "Tonight, was just a bit much for me. My dad seemed to overdo it a bit. There was no reasoning with him. I thought he was going to empty the wine cellar. I hope you understand. I'm just not accustomed to all that attention." Isaac stroked her arm and continued, speaking softly. "Look at me," he whispered softly as he lifted her chin to his. "You are my wife. You complete me. I'm happy you're in my life, and I know I'm truly blessed to have you."

He kissed her long and hard. She forgot her disappointment at leaving the celebration so early and enjoyed the moment that sealed her life as his wife.

That night, in the quiet serenity of their canopy bed, with the soft warm evening breeze billowing through the blue and gold sheer draped over their bed, Rebekah and Isaac became one.

CHAPTER 13

Twenty years passed quickly. In spite of their love making, which was always good and resulted in their being blessed with a set of twin boys, Isaac and Rebekah's communication was still sparse. She talked and he listened, but offered little-to-no feedback.

One afternoon, while searching for roses and, other decorative greenery from her garden, to decorate the house, Rebekah called her personal handmaid for assistance. Looking around, the handmaid pressed her hands to her cheeks and shook her head. "Ma'am, there isn't much to choose from, but I'll try to gather enough for a dining table decoration."

The scalding midday sun torched Rebekah's skin. She wiped away a bead of sweat that was on the verge of getting in her eye. "This has been an awfully dry season. In fact, I've had to personally water and watch one or two of these flower pots on a regular basis just to keep them alive." She tossed several dead flowers to the ground.

The maid shrugged and looked around. "The fruits and vegetables are struggling too. Everyone has been talking about the shortage of food in the area."

Rebekah rubbed her chin. "You know what? I think we need to have a gathering to lighten the mood around here. I'm sick of all this talk about a dry season. Our cellar is full and we need a distraction."

The handmaid laughed and carried the flower basket indoors, shaking her head. "I hope master Isaac is ready for this."

* * *

Rebekah entered her husband's office and, using the drawings and details outlined on several sheets of paper, she tried to make a case.

"We'll have food—in limited proportion—plenty of wine, and even a little music. I already have the handmaids preparing a list of items we have in the storage area. I just need the names of people you might like to invite to the gathering." She paused, taking in Isaac's body language, disapproving look, and change in countenance. Walking over, she leaned on his chair and rubbed his cheek. "Honey, what do you think? The focus is fellowship, not food. This will be a great way to band together, as community, and support one another."

Isaac tapped his fingers on the desk. Moving closer, she put her hand over his fingers to stop the impatient tapping and whispered. "We need something else to focus on other than when it will rain," she said while stroking the side of his face. "All I need from you is a list of who can be invited. I don't want to take a chance on inviting someone you don't approve of visiting our home. So, could you just do that for me? I promise that we'll use limited resources."

Isaac shifted in the chair, and raised his hand to interrupt her continued discussion. "Rebekah, I don't think this is a good idea," he said firmly. "It'll require a great deal of work on your part. And besides, I'm not sure anyone will be interested in attending." He rubbed his hands together. "As for a guest list, I don't have many friends here, and others are single men, who are busy merchants that live too far to travel for this kind of an event."

Rebekah moved away from Isaac. A flash of anger shot through her. With both hands on her hips, she paced the room. "What is it with you?" she shouted. "I've been here over two decades, and the most company we've had are your business associates and maybe one or two neighbors. I've put up with this semi-hermit lifestyle for a long time, but now I'm tired of it. I need some company other than our twins and you."

Leaning forward, she gave him a cool, piercing look. "How much conversation do you think I can have with teens?" I'm sick of the nothingness between me and you in our marriage. The only time I'm guaranteed your full attention is in bed. Isaac, my man, even that grows old."

Rebekah collected the papers she had been reviewing, and left on his desk. "I came to you with a simple plan to have a few adults over, as a way to take our minds off this dry season we're in right now. What I'm asking of you won't break the bank or deplete the pantry. It will, however, break your normal routine of avoiding the opportunity to socialize with people." With that last comment, she walked across the floor, dropped into a chair, and rubbed her hands together.

Isaac got up, moved away from his desk, jammed his hands in his pockets and stood in front of his wife. "I realize I don't talk to you about things happening around us like this drought. That's because I don't want to alarm you." He took her hand and stroked her fingers. "This famine is almost as bad as the one during my father's time. Things are worse than you've heard, and I apologize that I didn't make that clear to you sooner." He released her hand and stood back. "That's why I'm taking drastic action to protect our family."

She raised an eyebrow. "Meaning?"

Isaac lowered his eyes and shifted from one foot to the other. "We need to move. I haven't identified the exact time yet, but I've been able to work most things out. It'll be soon."

Rebekah almost laughed as she arose from her chair. "Soon," she shouted. "You withhold information from me for who knows how long, let me think everything is okay, maybe a little dryer than normal, but okay. Then the day I suggest we have a social gathering; you tell me we have to move." She hung her head and rocked back and forth. "How convenient is that!" With clinched fists, she stood, and she eyed her husband. "The last time I moved was a 'pack and go' to come here. As I remember, I didn't get much explanation or description of where we were going then. I don't plan to go through that again. Not after all these years married."

Isaac stepped close and reached to embrace his wife, but she pushed away.

"I prayed about it. We're moving to Gerar. It's a small town in Egypt," he said firmly. Walking back to a position near his desk, he added, "I heard from the Lord. If we—and we will obey—we'll be safe. We leave within the next few weeks." Isaac rubbed his hands together. "Rebekah, hear me. I don't want any discussions with or around the servants, and definitely not to any of our neighbors. We need to limit the possibility of panic. We'll only pack essentials and can purchase anything else we need when we get to Egypt."

Rebekah paused and studied the man who stood before her. "You say you heard from God on this matter? Is it that serious?"

Isaac returned to her side. This time she did not push away when he held her. "I ask that you trust that I heard from the Lord. We must leave. Our blessings await us in Gerar."

Rebekah, resigned to the move, was deep in the details of finalizing the household packing. After weeks of preparing, with very little assistance, she missed her mother and home. Their sons, having been told they would be going on an extended journey, were overly excited and had become unruly, fighting over every detail of the packing and she wanted a break. Rebecca approached her husband, again, about a detour visit to her mother.

"Isaac, since the boys are old enough to be helpful on the journey, why can't we stop at my mother's home on the way to Gerar? I've been away from my home now over twenty years," Rebekah told Isaac one evening, as she directed her handmaid to wrap and pack several dishes, she wanted to take on their journey. "My mother has visited only once since the boys were toddlers. I want her to have some time with them, before they're much older. We need to plan a visit, and this is a good time."

Isaac put the stack of documents on the table near his chair and stood, stretched, then moved toward the exit. "I have to check the servants' progress with several work projects I assigned."

Rebekah, threw a book in his direction. "That's how you avoid all conversations. No response. Silence and walk away. We never resolve issues, just set them aside in hopes they'll go away. Unfortunately, they never do. Well, I've already made arrangements for us to detour to my home town before moving to Gerar. And I expect you to travel with us."

Isaac paused in the doorway, raised his head to the ceiling and sighed. He turned to look at his wife. "Rebekah, we have been through this before. My family is to go to Egypt and stay, as the Lord told me. You and the boys are my family. When I hear from the Lord that it's safe to leave Gerar, then we'll plan a visit with your mother. I won't argue this point."

Opening the door to leave, Isaac was almost knocked to the floor when his son, Esau, slammed into his father's legs while racing his brother down the hall. Laughing, Isaac grabbed him around the neck. "After I confirm some things with the servants," he said to his wife. "I'll take Esau with me to the marketplace to pick up a few items."

Without a second glance at his other son, Jacob, who had been standing near his brother, Isaac left the room.

Rebekah frowned, then called to her son. "Jacob, baby, come with me to the pantry. I need help with the inventory." Looking down at the floor, shifting from side to side, he hesitated. She reached for Jacob and gave him a hug. "Come, help me with the inventory details and I'll fix you something special." Kissing him on the cheek, she whispered, "It is well, my son."

Isaac had his Esau and Rebekah had her Jacob.

* * *

In the weeks before the move to Gerar, Jacob and Esau were sent to the fields to harvest as much grain as they could find, in preparation for the move. This task would take a full day each time. One afternoon, Jacob decided to shorten his work day and prepare a meal of goat stew. When Esau arrived, after his day working in the fields, he was famished. He approached his brother, who was stirring the stew. The smell of the food made his stomach growl.

"Jacob, that looks good. Give me a bowl." Esau threw his tools aside, and sat next to his brother.

Jacob looked up smiled. "Get your own meal. This is for me." He proceeded to serve his bowl and eat. Esau was tired and too lazy to take time to fix his meal, and realized he had already eaten the nutcake and fish he brought with him from the pantry. There was nothing available for him but water.

Sliding closer, licking his lips he asked again. "Look brother, I'm hungry. What can I give you for a bowl of stew?

Jacob chuckled. "You must be really hungry to ask me that question. Are you really willing to give me anything for a bowl of stew?" He stopped stirring and looked his brother in the eyes. "Would you give me anything?"

Esau, grabbed an empty bowl and held it out for Jacob to fill. "Yes, anything. Now give me some of the food and stop playing around."

Jacob stood and looked in the fields for one of the manservants who had been working alongside them. Seeing one, he waved him over. Upon his arrival, the manservant was positioned so that he would hear the exchange. Jacob turned to his brother. "This day, Esau, I trade you this bowl of stew in for your birthright. By this exchange, I will now be recognized as firstborn. Do you agree?"

Esau laughed. "Yes. If it means that much to you, it is done. In exchange for a bowl of your stew, I give you, my brother Jacob, the right to be recognized as firstborn. I swear it this day."

Jacob turned to the manservant. "You heard this declaration from my brother?" The servant nodded. "Fine, you are dismissed." He turned back to Esau, and filled the bowl to the rim with goat stew. Esau ate every morsel in silence. When finished, he sneered at his brother. "They say you are always making deals. You sealed a deal today, didn't you?"

"You did what?!" Isaac shouted. He and Rebekah were on the patio when the boys returned from the fields. Esau and Jacob shared their covenant agreement with their father.

"This is incredible," Isaac responded, while glaring at Esau. "Well, son. It's clear where your priorities lie. It was your decision, and it's irrevocable. Let nothing more be said." He went into the house without another word. Esau followed behind in silence. Rebekah looked at Jacob and smiled. They sat quiet and enjoyed the sunset.

CHAPTER 14

Isaac, Rebekah, and their sons traveled to Gerar, no stopping to visit her mother, Milcah. They arrived to their new home unabated by any threats to their safety. The journey took several days through extremely dry areas, but the caravan was fully loaded with water, fruits, vegetables, and unleavened bread as their daily staples.

Though her young teens were excited about the journey, Rebekah had little use for the periodic sand storms and the hot sun. After four days, they reached their destination. Having already sent most of their handmaids and servants in advance of their arrival, nearly all the preparations for their new home were complete when the family got there.

"Just one stop to see my mother," she said while standing at the entrance to their tent and brushing dust from her dress. "That was the only request I made, yet you were obviously determined to ignore it. What would it have taken to go out of our way a few short kilometers for a short visit? But no. Face like flint, we had to come directly to Gerar." Waving her arms around then pointing at Isaac. "Well, we're here now, and I hope you're satisfied."

* * *

Needing a break, Rebekah sent the boys to the dining table for their evening meal and joined her husband on the patio. In spite of the sunset, the temperature was as warm and uncomfortable as midday. Rebekah sat in one of the comfortable pillow chairs. Feeling hot, she fanned her face, making as much noise as possible.

Isaac didn't appear to notice her arrival or movements. She poured water from the flask and set it on the table near his chair with a loud thud. "What do you think about having a gathering here? It would be a great way to introduce ourselves to the neighbors, and it would be great way for our guys to get acquainted with their neighbors."

Isaac paused, glanced at his wife, and grunted. "You mean Jacob would have an opportunity to meet new people." He continued reviewing the stacked of paperwork he had with him. "Esau doesn't have a problem making friends. He's always ready to interact with people, and never hesitates to enter a crowd."

Rebekah stood, walked over to Isaac's chair, and rested a hand on her hip. "What is it with you when it comes to Jacob? You give him as little attention as possible, while Esau could break your favorite chair and you'd sit with him to fix it. Let's see, could it be you're jealous because I appreciate the son who offers to help me, no matter what chore I have to do around here, or is the first to jump to go to the marketplace with me. Esau, on the other hand, literally runs at the site of work?"

Isaac shot a disgusted glance. "Esau loves the outdoors, and I for one will not fault him for it. I've taken him or several trips to observe the men when are out fishing and hunting. I invited both the boys. Jacob had no interest, so please don't speak to me about issues with the boys." He crossed his arms over his chest. "Now, I have a meeting tomorrow morning with King Abimelech, and there are several details that need to be addressed during these discussions."

Isaac returned his attention to the papers he was reviewing. "As I've said many times before, I realize this hasn't been easy for you and the boys. It was, however, necessary. In this family, God leads and we follow. The boys will adjust to the people and their environment, and make their own way, as it should be."

Rebekah shook her head and chuckled "As we have been led? You mean as *you* are led, don't you? I follow as you lead, even when it makes no sense. Even if it cost us our comfort, familiar surroundings, and friendships in our home land. Isn't that what you mean?"

Isaac stood and reached for her hand. "Come with me." She hesitated. He touched her shoulder. "Please." They walked down a short the steps of the patio to the path leading to their gardens. "Look. Out there."

Rebekah sighed and looked where her husband was pointing. The garden was lush with lilies, roses and greenery in full bloom. Isaac turned to his wife. "You have to admit, the view from our new home is much more promising than the conditions we left in our former home. This grass is green and our stock is being well fed."

Rebekah shrugged and turn to leave, but Isaac stopped her. "Listen, Rebekah. Can you hear the sounds in the marketplace?

There's much chatter and bartering taking place. That means business and prosperity. When we left Nahor, those sounds had died out because there were no crops or merchandise to sell." Rebekah didn't respond. The walk back to their patio was silent. She returned to the cushioned chair and sat quiet. Another battle lost.

In the silence that followed their walk, Isaac decided it was a good time to approach another issue that had been developing over the last few weeks. "Rebekah, I know you often journey to the marketplace." He moved his chair closer to his wife. "Well, I travel about the city too, and have been approached several times with questions about who you are. Actually, they ask whether or not you're my wife."

Rebekah chuckled. "I've noticed the men watching. So what? They ask you if I'm your wife. What's the issue? It's nice to know men still find me attractive after the hard time I had giving birth to these two boys," she responded while pointing toward the sounds of Esau and Jacob's voices outside in the area below the window. Isaac fell silent.

She gave him a side glance. "What is it Isaac?"

Smoothing his beard, he said, "You see, King Abimelech has also asked this question and I told him that you were my sister."

Rebekah jumped, shot him a look designed to peel his hide, and clinched her teeth. "Let me get this straight. You told the king that I was your sister?"

Isaac nodded, "And I told the men who questioned me in the marketplace the same thing."

Rebekah raised her hand and, for the first time in their marriage, slapped her husband across the face. "What in God's heaven would lead you to do such a thing?! Your sister? I'm now your sister? What was it this time? Were you visited in a dream again?" she shouted.

Isaac looked at the ceiling as if searching for an answer.

Rebekah folded her arms and grunted. "All this time I've been in the marketplace shopping, and these men think I'm your sister?"

Isaac reached for his wife but she pushed away.

"Rebekah, I had to do it. You're so beautiful that I thought if I told anyone you were my wife; they might kill me because they wanted you."

She whirled around, "And any one of them might take me because they think I'm unwed." Rebekah returned to the chair and sat down again. She started to laugh and cry at the same time. "You brought us to this strange land. You share little of your thoughts. You make decisions without discussing anything with me. You decide you're the expert, and you know what's best in each situation."

She extended her index finger toward him and smirked. "You certainly have bitten off quite a mouthful this time, my husband."

Rebekah covered her face and sighed. "Because I know so little of this land and its people, I'll lean on your discretion in this matter, and live here as your sister. I'm just too tired to fight your reasoning, and clearly, we can't change the story now."

Rebekah walked to the patio door without looking at her husband. Before entering the house, she paused. "Hear me on this, Isaac. From now on, you must travel with me to the marketplace. I won't go there again with only a handmaid."

Rebekah and Isaac lived for some time under the deception about their relationship. She was his sister in public and his wife behind closed doors. Walking through the crowded marketplace with her "brother," she nodded and smiled while mumbling, "This is your idea of the good life? I hate every moment of this pretense. You've created a mess of this marriage, Isaac. Tell me, what do you plan to do when one of these men asks to visit and sit with me?"

Isaac continued to stroll with her, carrying their packages while waving and smiling at the men tending their merchandise. "We'll straighten this out soon," he muttered, squeezing his wife's hand. I'll gradually make them aware. You'll see. It'll be all right."

Rebekah stopped walking. Stalls loaded with fruits and vegetables, cloth and meat lined the street on both sides as far as she could see. It was a busy market day, so the crowds packed the area. Everything was joyful and lively. Under normal circumstances, she would have enjoyed the activities. Unfortunately, there was still the lie that separated them in the marriage. Looking up, while strolling, she searched Isaac's face. The sun was so bright, she squinted and was forced to use her hands to shade her eyes. Anyone observing would think she was asking her brother a question.

"Isaac," Rebekah whispered. "How can you expect me to respect you? You aren't even man enough to tell these men,"—she pointed around the area— "that I am your wife. What kind of man have I married?"

Before responding, Isaac quickly looked around, hoping no one had heard his wife. "We can discuss this further at home, don't you think?" Touching her arm gently, he proceeded to guide her through the crowd. "Let's finish the shopping."

Rebekah didn't respond. She glared at him with disgust, and proceeded through the marketplace.

Shopping completed, Rebekah and Isaac started for home, in silence. When they reached the gated entrance, the silence was more than Isaac could bear. Without thinking, he reached for his *sister*. "Rebekah, you know I love you." Isaac caressed her back and arms gently while hugging her close. "Give me just a little more time here with these people. I'll fix this issue, I promise."

He kissed her gently on the cheek.

Rebekah breathed heavily and hugged him firmly. They entered the house for an evening together—as man and wife.

"What? You're lying. That man didn't pass his wife off as his sister. You need to stop." The other two handmaids laughed.

Rebekah's personal attendant, nodded. "It's true. These poor folks moved here, and all the men are sniffing behind mistress, and she's pretending not to notice." Pounding the dough she was working on in preparation for the honey buns needed for dinner, she chuckled. "We gotta help them out. No talking about this issue. Do you hear me? No backyard over-the-fence exchange of details. If they get found out, it could be bad for all of us. I don't know about you, but I'm not interested in returning to that dry spot we just left."

Wiping her hands on the nearest towel, Rebekah's personal attendant looked around the kitchen and reinforced the commitment. "All mouths shut, subject over." After a moment of silence, she continued. "Great, now let's get this dinner prep over with." She rubbed her stomach, "Once they've finished eating, we can eat, and I'm hungry."

CHAPTER 15

"Bring him here! Immediately," King Abimelech bellowed. "He had just returned from enjoying a walk on his balcony, something he did daily alone.

His servant bowed. "Sire, you want the man Isaac here now?"

The king turned quickly and glared at his servant. "What? Has my language changed? Is there something you don't comprehend? I want the man Isaac in my chambers and I want him here now!" The servant bowed again and left.

While waiting for Isaac, the king's chief counsellor knocked and entered with papers requiring the king's review and signature. He placed the papers on the desk.

Abimelech pushed the stack away. "I have no time for these now." Rubbing his beard, he motioned for his chief counsellor to sit. "Tell me, what do you know of this man Isaac?"

The king's counselor shrugged and scratched his head. "Nothing in particular, Sire. He appears to be a man with good administrative skills and business integrity. I have had no issues with him, and have heard nothing to suggest he is not a man to be trusted in the marketplace. He has a good reputation in the region, as well. Is something wrong?"

The king tapped his finger. "For months, I've been led to believe the woman Rebekah was his sister, but I observed something today that leads me to believe otherwise. I have commanded his presence to answer these suspicions, and I expect the truth."

* * *

"Hey Dad, did you see this? East entered his father's office with his catch for the day, with his mother trailing behind.

"Esau, look at you!" she shouted while holding a cloth under the dripping fish, "Get this mess to the kitchen. You're ruining the floors that the handmaids just cleaned."

Isaac laughed and grabbed his favorite son's shoulders. "Great catch. Now go, before your mother gets even more upset. Take these things to the kitchen."

Esau left the room, ignoring his mother's glance.

Rebekah threw the smelly cloth on the floor. "Here, you clean it up. No matter what that boy does, you find a way to reward his behavior either by something you say or do. He doesn't even acknowledge me unless absolutely necessary."

Isaac picked up the cloth and placed it on a stool near the window. "I'll have one of the servants take care of the floors, Rebekah. Any stains or odors will be gone before dinner. As for Esau's relationship with you, Isaac responded, as he closed the door to his study. Could it be your obvious favoritism to Jacob that's created Esau's indifference?"

Rebekah tossed her head with a half laugh. "We both know Esau was always your choice." Grabbing the door handle, she tossed a last comment over her shoulder. "As for Jacob, he has always been there to help me. He maintains every aspect of the home operations and you know it. It's you who created the divide between the boys. When you tossed Jacob aside, he knew I would be there for him. And I am."

Before Rebekah could turn the door handle, it was opened from the other side.

"Excuse me ma'am," her handmaid said and bowed. "A messenger from the palace is here for master Isaac."

Rebekah took one last look at her husband. "Duty calls," she snapped, then pushed past her handmaid and left the room.

When Isaac entered the great hall of the palace, he was greeted and escorted to the King's quarters by two guards. Upon entering, he noticed the chief counsellor seated in a corner near the wall of books, artifacts, and papers. He nodded to Isaac, but didn't smile. The king was seated at a large desk with his manservant arranging a tray of melon, figs, grapes, and olives, in addition to several flasks of wine perched on one of the tables close to the king's desk.

As Isaac approached the king's desk, the manservant stepped forward and bowed. "Sir, there's a chair over here for your convenience."

Before Isaac could acknowledge the servant's comment, the King looked up from his paperwork, and responded. "It's not necessary. He will stand."

Isaac stood for several moments. King Abimelech kept his head buried in his work.

"Sire," Isaac said. "You summoned me. How may I be of assistance?"

The King placed his reed pen firmly on the desk, raised his eyes to look directly at Isaac. Leaning back, he tapped his fingers on the arm of the chair. It was a magnificent piece of furniture with an engraved design on its high back, accented by enormous royal blue cushions with gold trim.

Isaac shifted from one foot to the other.

Leaning forward in his chair and, using his pen, the king pointed at Isaac. "You told me the woman Rebekah was your sister. Is that correct?"

Isaac looked at the chief counsellor, then back at the king. Standing erect, with both arms behind his back, he nodded "Yes, Sire. That is correct I told you Rebekah was my sister.

The king threw the pen on the desk. "Yet I saw you rubbing and kissing her while you were in the yard outside of your home. These were not the actions of a brother to his sister." King Abimelech glanced at his chief counsellor then moved from behind his desk. He walked toward Isaac. "She isn't your sister. She's your wife, is that not correct?"

Isaac cleared his throat and responded in a low tone. "Yes, Sire. Rebekah is my wife."

"Why would you do this?" he shouted, clinching his fist. "One of my men could have slept with her, causing great trouble in my country. This is unacceptable behavior. You came to us to live in greater prosperity, and now you do this."

Isaac waited for the king to finish, then offered his explanation. "Sire, I deceived everyone because I was afraid, I might be killed if another man wanted her. I realize this was the wrong decision on my part, and humbly ask your forgiveness. I just didn't know what else to do. We're new to this country, and I attempted to negotiate the challenge the best way I knew how. Apparently, it was the wrong way. Please forgive the error. I in no way wanted to offend you or put your men in a compromising situation."

King Abimelech walked back to his chair and sat down. He poured a cup of wine and leaned back, then turned and nodded to his chief chancellor. "Please get my scribe."

The chancellor left and returned immediately with a man carrying a scroll made of papyrus and the reed pen.

"This is my command. Write it word for word," the King announced. "Be it so ordered that anyone who so much as lays a single hand on Isaac or Rebekah will be put to death."

The king signed the order, and commanded it be read aloud in the district, then have it posted in the marketplace, among troops, and all other areas throughout the region.

The king turned his attention to Isaac. "Now you, Isaac, and your wife are free to live and work the land without fear. No one will bother you."

Isaac bowed. "Thank you, my king. I appreciate your understanding and support."

After Isaac left, the king turned to his counsellor. "What a foolish man."

* * *

Isaac and his family lived well in the land. They prospered through planting crops and growing flocks and herds that were blessed by God. He became a very rich man, so rich it provoked the king to jealousy. As a result, Isaac was called once again to meet with the king.

"You have become too rich, too powerful," the king said as he reviewed the report of Isaac's holdings provided to him by his scribe. "This is not good. I want you to leave. Take your family, your flocks and herds, and your servants, and leave my country."

When Isaac told Rebekah the news, she received it with a resignation of what she believed was one more issue Isaac created. "How many times must I remind you that communication makes the difference."

Throwing items in a packing case, she paused, shrugged then continued. "Maybe if you had offered to share our prosperity with the king, by making him a partner in the businesses, we wouldn't have to be packing to move again. Oh no, you didn't do that. Instead the king gets jealous because he thinks we may become better off than he is, and now we have to leave. He probably thinks we were hoarding stuff. Isaac, no communication means no trust."

Rebekah stopped packing and sat on a nearby chair. "Esau and Jacob are young adults now. We need to settle down so they can be established in a new life in preparation for their future."

Isaac chuckled. "You mean we need to get settled so Jacob can establish new operations for his future, don't you? He was known for wheeling and dealing in our old place. That boy has a nose for opportunities—as long as he doesn't have to get his hands dirty."

Rebekah decided not to let Isaac provoke her by getting into the Jacob and Esau comparison. "You just don't seem to get it. Just because Esau likes to hunt and fish, doesn't mean he is better than the one who uses his intelligence and wit in other ways. I'm just making sure we stabilize to ensure their future, with no one having more attention or benefit than the other."

The move to yet another new location created an even greater divide between Isaac and Rebekah. Bickering and arguments escalated to the point that Rebekah chose to live in separate quarters at their new location. "There is no love left between us, Isaac, and I prefer the quiet of my own space."

Isaac, never wanting confrontation and always seeking to avoid negative discussions and disagreements as much as possible, eagerly agreed to the separate sleeping arrangements.

Years passed and Isaac grew more and more successful, gaining great wealth. Unfortunately, his marriage was in shambles, and fierce competition between his sons escalated. Esau had grown more rebellious, choosing to live his life the complete opposite of his father's wishes. This selfish behavior resulted in his marrying two Hittite women—against the established laws of his faith—and moving them to live with Rebekah and Isaac, creating an even more miserable situation for the family.

"If you could just keep your voices down when having your discussions," Rebekah shouted, while leveling a glaring look at Esau, as she entered the suite rooms assigned to him and the wives. "The entire household does not need to hear your arguments."

Esau's wives glared at Rebekah, but stood watching her in silence. They had learned early on that disrespect to the mistress of the house would not be tolerated. As long as they were civil to her, they were assured a roof over their heads. All in all, they had the run of the house, and made full use of it.

Rebekah turned her attention to Isaac. "Your father is getting older. These daily flare ups and late-night visitors, with loud noise every other night, are not good for him. For his sake, if not mine, please control these activities. Esau, did not look at his mother. He just nodded to let her know he heard what she said.

A flash of anger rushed through her, as she walked over to her son, put her hand under his chin and raised it so that he was looking at her. "I need you to get a handle on your family and your activities while living in the house and I need you to do this now. You continue making poor choices while your father defends your right to mess up. You have to be here." She raised her arm and pointed in the direction of the wives. "But they don't."

Esau glowered at her, and spoke through clinched teeth. "Mother, as long as father is living, I can bring whomever I choose here. I've already proven that. We've never had much to say to each other. No point in starting now." He moved her hand and continued focusing on what he was doing.

Rebecca turned to leave. "Mother," Esau called out. "Please let the servants know we expect guests tonight for dinner. My wives and I will entertain them on the patio, so they should prepare that area. That way, you, Jacob and father can eat your quiet meal in the dining room."

Rebecca didn't acknowledge her son had spoken. She opened the door and left. "God help us if any children come out of this arrangement," she mumbled.

CHAPTER 16

"Get off it, man," Esau answered in response to Jacob's accusation that he manipulated the affection and favoritism of his dad. "You're the apple of mom's eye," he snapped. "She's done everything for you, and you got the best of anything that rolled through here."

Jacob laughed. "You're just angry because you chose to trade your birthright to relieve your hunger pains. That's not my problem. All you had to do was take extra time and fix your own meal. But thank you, my brother. Because of your poor decision, I now inherit the leadership and authority of dad, at his death. Get that in your head and accept it."

Jacob grabbed some figs off the table, and flopped down on the couch. "Besides, I'm already running most of the operations now anyway; so why don't you just keep on hunting, my man. Enjoy yourself." He gestured with his thumb, then popped another fig in his mouth and gave his brother a broad smile.

Esau stormed out of the room to search for his father. He found him sitting on the patio, enjoying the warmth of the sun. The cool breeze refreshed the old man. Age had caught up to him. His eyes were failing and he couldn't move around without assistance. In spite of his plight, he was peaceful and relaxed. Life had been good to him. He was a rich man and had a son to share his wealth.

"Dad, I need to talk to you," Esau said as he rushed over to sit with him. He shared the incident that happened between he and his brother earlier, with Jacob taunting him over the fact he sold his birthright for a bowl of stew. "He caught me at a weak moment, father. It is unfair that I should be forced to keep this covenant. Can't you do something?

Isaac turned toward Esau's voice. "Son, you chose to make an agreement with your brother. You were both old enough then to know what you were doing. I was not consulted, before the decision was reached, and cannot violate tradition by overriding what has already been done." Esau banged the table in frustration.

Isaac shook his head and held up his hand for silence. "You know I don't approve of such outbursts. Calm yourself. Nothing is worth losing self-control, remember that." Leaning forward and smiling, he said, "Go now and fetch me some fresh meat, and I will bless you with the blessing only I can provide."

Jumping from the chair, Esau laughed, hugged his dad, and ran off to kill fresh meat for a meal for his father.

Little did either Esau or Isaac know, Rebekah was listening to the conversation, and overheard details of the plan Isaac had for his favorite child. She searched for Jacob and found him in the pantry area.

"Son," she whispered. Your father is about to perform the inheritance ritual for your brother. Come with me. We must make plans and move swiftly."

As they walked toward the lower level pantry area, Rebekah shared with him what she had heard her husband tell Esau. "Your father plans to convey the ultimate blessing on your brother, but your father's eyesight is very poor. It's worse than even you and Isaac are aware." Rebekah pulled Jacob closer to ensure no one would hear their conversation. "I have a plan, my son."

Retrieving the long bow from the storage cupboard in the pantry, she handed it to her son. "Go kill and skin a sheep, and bring the skin to me. Do it now. We don't have a moment to waste."

Jacob did as he was told. While he was gone, Rebekah had the servants move Isaac to his lounge chair in his room. Evening had come, and the lighting was dimmer. She also ensured there would be only one torch burning at the far end of the room.

"Send Esau to me as soon as he returns, Isaac admonished his servant." Rebekah nodded to the servant who spoke directly to Isaac. "Yes, sire. I will let him know you are waiting in your room."

When Jacob returned, Rebekah gave him further instructions. "Listen carefully, Jacob. Your brother is very hairy, and your skin is smooth. We have to make your father believe he's talking to Esau when this covenant ritual is performed." She wiped the blood from the sheepskin. "Here, cover both your arms with this so that the wool will fool your father into thinking he's touching your brother's hairy arms. If this works like I think it will, your father will pronounce the ultimate blessing on you instead of Esau. It's a blessing that cannot be rescinded once given."

Rebekah hugged her son. "Go now. Perform this task, and your future will be secure. You earned it and you *deserve* it."

When Jacob entered his father's, he found him leaning back in his lounge chair, covered with a light blanket. As Jacob entered, he ensured he approached him from the shadows. Following the instructions from his mother, Jacob had covered his arms with the skin from the freshly-killed sheep and entered his father's room. "Esau, my son," Isaac smiled. "You've returned." Jacob didn't respond. Isaac raised his arms for an embrace.

Jacob sat at his father's side and placed his hairy arms around him. At that moment, one of the manservants entered the room, sent by Rebekah to witness the ceremony, he stood silent. Assured that his favorite son was in his presence, Isaac performed the inheritance ritual.

Esau returned from the hunt his father requested, and the details of what happened in his absence were exposed. "What have you done, father? He paced back and forth, cursing and throwing pillows across the room. "Mother has always found a way to control or manipulate situations. Now she's won the ultimate prize for her favorite son." He leaned close to his father and grabbed his hand. "Can you hear me now father? Do you know it's me, your son Esau? Isaac reached for his son, but Esau pushed him away. "You've given my future away."

The venom and hostility between the brothers continued, under threats of violence, until the situation was out of control. At one point, Esau threatened to kill his brother for stealing his inheritance. In addition to their own bickering, his wives kept the pot of dissension stirring at every opportunity. With the situation beyond reconciliation on any level, Isaac and Rebekah agreed Jacob should leave and make a new life in the country of Rebekah's brother, Laban—some 400 miles away.

At bequest of his parents, Jacob left his home to sojourn to his new life with his uncle Laban. And so, began the story of Rachel, Leah, and Jacob.

COMMENTARY

Isaac was not an argumentative young man, and he never doubted his father's decisions or choices. Even as a child, he submitted to his father's instructions to be tied like a fatted calf prepared for slaughter. Only by his father's determination and faith was Isaac's life changed. With full knowledge that his son needed a strong woman to support and encourage him, Abraham's plans included ensuring his son's wife would not only be a woman of faith, but one strong enough to move his son in the right direction. Clearly this was accomplished through prayer resulting in Isaac marrying a woman of strong character and with great communication skills.

The challenge in the marriage between Isaac and Rebecca was that he was an introvert, quite happy living a life away from unnecessary contact with people, while his wife was a communicator, eager to connect with people and socialize. In modern day times, marriage counseling may have helped this couple overcome the challenges, by introducing information about behavioral styles and how each could respect the other's differences, the success of which would have resulted in their living happily ever after.

Unfortunately, that was not the case. So, Rebekah grew miserable in her loneliness, moving from place to place, never connecting with others and cementing wholesome relationships.

Historical narratives suggest Isaac never fully understood why Rebekah wasn't satisfied with him. From his perspective, all the comforts of life were provided. In addition to his physical need, all he wanted was to be respected as the man of the house. Because neither of had been fulfilled by the other, they chose to live their lives through their children. In the course of time, this launched a competition over which parent would provide more love and affection for their chosen son. It's unfortunate that all these issues resulted, because this couple wasn't successful accomplishing an important level of care and affection for each other. It's a sad ending to what could have been a great love story.

STORY THREE: HOUSEWIVES OF MESOPOTAMIA: RACHEL, LEAH, AND JACOB

CHAPTER 17

"Even if it was written in scripture long ago,
you can be sure it's written for us."
— Romans 15:4

Rachael stormed out of the family gathering, then glared at her father. "You've got to be kidding me. What are you saying?"

Laban's eyebrows winged upward at her tone. She had never been disrespectful, though he did realize she was clearly upset. Understandable, since he had just given her a slight bit of bad news. Well, maybe more than bad. More along the lines of ... devastating. At least for her.

"Jacob is *my* fiancé, betrothed to me. You allowed that," she shrieked, thumping a hand to her chest. "He is *my* man and you expect me to just turn him over to Leah, with her spoiled self, because she couldn't find a man for herself?" She waved her hand in a dismissive fashion. "Haven't I shared enough with her? Before you became rich, it was my bedroom. My clothes. Now my man? Really? Where do they do that at?"

Laban sighed, dropped on the sofa in their quarters. Running a hand over his short-cropped hair, he hoped her need to blow off steam would end soon. Especially since she had slipped into a little slang at the end. His daughter was highly educated. They didn't do slang in their house. His wife would normally be the one to put his daughters in check, but this was a special circumstance. So much so, that he was sweating like one of the slaves he owned. Sad, because he was actually Hebrew. And with their Kosher diet ... they had a healthier constitution than most. But that was another story for another time.

"This is some mess." Rachel walked toward the family portrait on the mantle, glaring at the beauty who looked more like Adinah, her mother, with smooth chocolate skin, full lips, long slender legs, and wide hips. Rachel took after his side of the family, all long legs and svelte stature. "Just exactly what do you expect me to do now, father? How about I give her an arm and a leg while I'm at it? At least I have two of those. Since she's always aiming to have more than her fair share."

Laban stood, maneuvered past the large cushions and bright tapestry, then paced the area, contemplating his next words as his daughter's voice echoed throughout their home. He was very aware, if he couldn't convince Rachel of the value of this decision, all would be lost. He would be embarrassed among the elders of the town. His oldest daughter was waiting in the wings, while the youngest daughter was set to be married. Rachel knew the laws. She must see the wisdom in waiting. That break of tradition would not be tolerated.

He checked the shadow clock and continued measuring time via the sixty second intervals. The longest he'd ever seen Rachel go in was about ten minutes. But this situation suggested she was going to run an angry marathon. He returned to the sofa, realizing he might be there long past dinner. His stomach grumbled in protest.

* * *

The scent of lamb smothered in onions, garlic, and date honey, along with the aroma of fresh baked bread, made his stomach turn loops hours later, but he had tasted none. Instead, everything was spread out on the dinner table on the lower level, getting cold. His wife had taken a seat on the large pillows, watching everything unfold. Laban realized that Rachel was finally running out of steam. If he thought his wife could go in, Rachel had her beat, hands down. He untied the waist tassel then placed his blazer on the arm of the sofa.

"Daughter," Laban gently responded. "Hear me. This is only *one part* of my plan. After the marriage is consummated, I will offer Jacob the option to marry you also. In that way, we will not have broken tradition and you will still have Jacob as your husband." He lowered his voice, adding after a quick glance at his wife, "Eventually."

Rachel stood in the center of the parents' suite. The enclosure somehow seemed smaller, congested, and cluttered, though everything was tidy and in its place. Rachel's anger was taking up most of the space. She seemed to sense her mother's dark brown eyes watching her every move.

"So, this is what you're offering me? A *delayed* ceremony! When we've done all this planning and everything? Invitations were done in handwritten Calligraphy art in preparation for my wedding. The invites already went out, all the way to Harran and Canaan. And now you want to make me second string, as though I'm just coming off the bench when I've been in the game since the first quarter?" She shook her head, the headwrap coming loose enough that her hair touched down to her shoulders. "So, when, pray tell, father, had you planned for *my* ceremony to take place? Next week? Two weeks from now? When?"

Before her father could respond, Rachel pivoted suddenly— almost as if she just remembered her mother was in the room. She clenched her teeth and tightened her fists in an effort to control her tone. It must have taken everything in her not to scream her next words. "And you mother, how long have you known of this plan for my sister to marry my man? Did everybody know but me? Did you tell my sister? The handmaids? The housekeeper? All the details I worked into my plans. Now, nothing." Rachel fell silent, staring at her mother, desperately seeking support.

Laban's wife averted her gaze to the carpet to avoid her daughter's angry glare. *Some help she is.*

"No, my precious daughter." Her father reached for her hand, but she pulled away. "We must give it some time so that it does not appear to be ... *an illegitimate* plan. People must not wonder if Jacob's marriage to Leah was authentic. I was thinking, perhaps, waiting ..." He put a few feet of distance between them. "Another ... hmmm." He glanced at his wife, who simply blinked several times and folded her arms across her chest. "Oh, let's say ... seven years."

Seven years?!

Rachel stared long and hard at her father. She had lived with him long enough to observe how he interacted with people when he was plotting to get something he wanted. She was aware of his reputation and label as "the master of impostors." Her fiancée, Jacob, had made good money for him in the last seven years he had stayed with them. The man had shown he was good stock the moment he helped increase profits for Laban in the sheep tending business. Laban had grown substantially rich. No need for the sisters to share a room any more. They now had servants, handmaidens, and more.

She knew, from the moment she spotted Jacob when she was watering her father's flock, that there was potential for him to marry her, move away, and start life on their own—totally away from her controlling and manipulative father. He'd already wrapped several businesses in his snare with his penchant for managing the house of Bethuel, his mother's brother. Thanks to Jacob's many years of service, they now owned fertile farmland, cattle, sheep, and a host of other agriculture-related companies that kept them well situated.

Rachel heard her parents discussing Jacob's challenges with his family many times. So, duping a foreigner with a past, who obviously was running from something or someone, was a piece of fig cake. In fact, Rachel was eager to get out from under the influence of her father, and she knew he was totally aware of that unfortunate fact. She saw this move for exactly what it was—Jacob taking Leah as his first wife then marrying Rachel afterward was a way of keeping them all under his thumb.

Rachel stood near the living area entrance, unable to keep the tears from flowing and her heart from breaking. "So, this is the real issue, isn't it, father? I have to buy my way to freedom from you and save you from the embarrassment at the same time? Where's the fairness in that?"

Laban locked gazes with his wife, whose lips were set in a thin, disapproving line. She picked up the white linen wedding gown and busied herself with the finishing touches on its embroidered trim. Rachel paused and casually approached. "Careful mother, she sneered. We wouldn't want a seam to burst in the wrong area, that would expose that deceitful witch." Adinah shook her head but didn't look up.

Turning to her father with curled lips and clinched fists, Rachel leaned forward. "You want me to participate in this charade and, for my silence, I will be free from you forever, right?"

The silence in the living quarters of was so tense, even the housekeeper and chefs dared not enter.

"Our family has already endured one scandal," Laban whispered. "What scandal?" She tilted her head in his direction. "I didn't do anything. Neither did Leah."

Laban rubbed his hands together and licked his lips. "Well, that whole thing with Esau and Jacob," he said with a weary sigh.

Rachel threw her head back and glared at her father. "Esau and Jacob are our cousins. Their feud has nothing to do with us." She crossed her arms. "So why am I suddenly paying the cost for you to remain the boss?"

Laban went to the window and gazed out at the fertile fields. A man did not get to be in the position in which he was in unless he'd plotted, schemed, and manipulated people and property. Jacob had demonstrated he was intelligent, skilled and extremely resourceful for a man who had moseyed into town with nothing more than a few shekels, a garment on his shoulders, and the wind on his back. Laban knew Jacob was hiding something, but had been unable to get him to confide. He kept his cards close to the chest, but two could play that game. Another seven years of labor to cover the bride price of his younger daughter. Fair exchange; ain't no highway robbery.

"Daughter, do this for me," he said, coming to stand near her. "And I will make things right for you. I promise."

CHAPTER 18

L eah lounged on the veranda of their spacious house, listening to the heated exchange. Laban had already told her the plan long before he'd tipped his hand to Rachel.

Probably knowing her baby sister was going to hit the roof and nearly cause it to go up in flames.

As soon as Leah learned about Rachel's impending marriage, she whined and complained to her mother and father, emphasizing her fear of never marrying. The pickings were slim in the area they lived. The numbers were nearly ten women to one man. So, having a perfectly healthy, handsome, and very available man stroll in out of the blue was like a gift from God. The fact that he was her cousin didn't complicate things. It just meant no background check was needed.

When her initial arguments hadn't worked, she had appealed to her father on the grounds of Hebrew law and custom. *Jackpot!*

The best part of the plan was how they were going to pull one over on Jacob. He would definitely not go for this, since he only had eyes for Rachel. Wouldn't even give Leah a first, second, or third look. *That scoundrel!* Thank God for Hebrew laws. The oldest marries first. And thanks to Jacob's mother encouraging him to leave home for a while, she reeled in a man that helped to double the amount of property, assets, and money their family had.

The day of the ceremony, the custom of wearing a veil so the bride's face is fully covered would serve the right purpose—to hide the fact that Laban had pulled a fast—and a slow one. The scheme allowed Laban to make good on his promise to have his oldest daughter marry first, while soothing his youngest daughter with a promise of getting the man she wanted later, if she would cooperate. All this without a hitch. Well, only a small one. *Would Rachel ever shut up?*

Leah had some of the beautiful attributes of Rachel, except for that unfortunate challenge with her left eye. It refused to move in concert with the other eye, creating an unattractive distraction when anyone spoke to her. Because of this and all the other issues, now more than ever, she was glad for a custom that requires the couple maintain their distance on what was supposed to be the happiest day of her life.

From the parts of the discussion she was able to overhear, Leah was confident her father had fixed the issue. She could now prepare to be married to this handsome—and now rich—man, a prize she could never have won on her own. *Why put in that work, when you can reap the benefits of someone else's hard labor. The Egyptians had that down to a science.*

As Leah quietly reveled in the triumph of being able to marry Jacob, she focused on how to alter that wedding garment her mother had been working on. In the middle of her thoughts, Rachel walked in. Leah schooled her features so that her expression seemed sorrowful, as if she shared her sister's pain. Nothing could be further from the truth.

"Well, I see you and father have worked out details for your marriage to *my man*," Rachel said, her voice dripping with sarcasm. "You are one despicable woman."

Leah widened her eyes, placed a trembling hand over her bosom. "Who me? I don't know what you're talking about."

Rachel kicked the door closed. "No matter what I have had in my life, you always thought you deserved part, if not all, of it. Let me tell you, you aren't woman enough for Jacob—you ugly slant-eyed heifer." She stabbed a finger in Leah's chest. "You may have won round one, but know this, Leah: in the end, I will win."

"Maybe," Leah shot back, angered at her sister's words. "We'll see. Seven years is a long way from now, though."

Rachel's dark brown eyes flashed fire. With that final remark, Rachel threw a pillow to the floor, walked over to the large tray of fruit and cheese Leah had left from lunch, grabbed a bunch of grapes and the cheese knife. Slowly, she began to peel each grape with the sharp knife. Her act was so slow and deliberate, almost as if she were imagining something—or someone else.

Leah became uncomfortable and tipped out of the room before her sister traded a grape for her head.

The day of Leah's ceremony, Rachel awoke after having endured a restless night, only to add the insult of sounds of people scurrying around, going from bedroom to bedroom, gathering items in preparation for the wedding.

Her mother slowly opened the bedroom door, carrying a tray of fruits and freshly baked bread. "Daughter, I brought you something to eat. I noticed the breakfast tray delivered to you at dawn was returned with your having barely touched the food."

Rachel turned over from her face-down position on the bed and glared at her mother. "Why, thank you, my dear sweet mom. You're such a ray of sunshine on this dark day. Just put the tray on the table and please leave as quietly as you entered. I don't want to see or talk to anyone this day. Especially the people who betrayed me— including you."

Adinah slammed the fruit tray on the dressing table and glared at her daughter as if she didn't know who this person was. "Alright, Rachel," she whispered. Her downturned mouth was an indication that she was keeping her anger at bay lest they argue and bring down the spirit of the household. "I get it. This is not the best situation. The deck has been stacked. The game is in play. But your turn will come."

"That's not good enough! I deserve—"

A loud clap of Adinah's hands and a stern "Shhh!" made Rachel stop short.

Adinah peered at her daughter. "I realize that aggressiveness is an asset for a shepherdess like you. Defending a herd is no easy task. But you are not in the field now and you are not in charge." She marched to the bed and took Rachel's chin in her hand. "Let this be the last disrespectful word you say to me, young lady or we will take this to another level. Do you hear me?!"

Rachel sat up straighter in the bed, eyes wide. "Yes mother." "That's my girl." Her mother paused, looked straight into her eyes, then crossed the room, shut the door quietly and was gone.

Unlike the original wedding plans, Rachel had sent notice to her girlfriends that they wouldn't be needed as bridesmaids because she and Jacob were going to have a more private ceremony.

Unfortunate, but necessary. Having your husband stolen right before your eyes did have its disadvantages. Now stealing someone else's husband? That was an entirely different Commandment altogether.

Rachel glanced at the tray her mother left for her. She scanned the room as a soft cool breeze blew the sheer curtains ever so lightly. She almost went to the window but didn't for fear someone might observe her movements. Her father made it clear she was not to be seen by *anyone*, except the handmaids delivering her food. No one, until the wedding was over.

She pulled the bed covers closer to her bosom, then planted her head in the pillow so it would muffle the sounds of her crying.

Laban opened the door to his changing room, prepared to leave for the ceremonies. He was surprised to see Rachel standing on the other side. "My daughter, I thought we agreed you would stay in your bedroom suite for the duration of the ceremony and celebration."

Rachel avoided her father's look of pity and let her gaze follow the lines on the floor just beyond the doorway. She smoothed the inner folds of her night gown and was embarrassed when she realized she wasn't wearing any sandals. She had run to her parents' suites barefooted. Finally gaining enough courage, she returned her father's gaze. "I don't intend to spoil your plans, father, but I need you to arrange for me to leave here—immediately. I need to be away for a while."

He inhaled sharply, but before he could get a word in, she continued. "You see, that seven-year deal you forced on me didn't take into account that I would be left watching another woman enjoying an intimate relationship with my man. I can't stay here and watch this horror story unfold."

Rachel walked over to the window near her father's desk. "I need you to arrange for me to stay with my grandparents for a few years. I'll return as we get closer to my wedding to Jacob, but I don't intend to stay here and let Leah flaunt her marriage in front of me for the next seven years. That's just not happening."

Laban paced the floor flailing his arms in disgust at Rachel's suggestions. "You can't possibly mean what you are saying. You are important to the family business operations and, of course, we would miss you." He stopped pacing and walked toward his daughter with caution. Laban took his daughter's hand. A broad smile creeped across his face as he spoke.

"Rachel, I have an idea that will maintain our tradition and, I believe, will also make you very happy. The ceremony for Leah and Jacob will proceed according to plan. Then we will proceed with plans for your nuptials. Of course, we will need to wait an appropriate amount of time to ensure there are no unfortunate discussions among the brethren. Let's say one week, shall we?" He hugged her close. "Yes, that's right, we can proceed with your marriage to Jacob in one week."

Rachel repelled the embrace, stepped back, and spent several seconds in silence while studying her father's face. She is well versed in his moods and motions when negotiating and searched for one hint of deceit, but found none. She sighed heavily and began to pace the floor.

"Alright, father. I accept the arrangement, but I still want to leave in the morning. I will return within six days to finalize plans for my wedding ceremony." Rachel was aware that her absence even for this short time period would ensure her father would not change his mind and attempt to worm his way out of the promise to her. Laban needed her, and being away from the business chores any length of time would reaffirm that fact for him. Rachel also intended to return with her new gown and extravagant wedding trimmings, that would go far beyond anything Leah had planned for her wedding. She was a favorite of her grandparents. She was sure they would help her make this happen.

Frustrated, Laban sat quiet in his chair, and opened his mouth to protest. Rachel raised her hand to stop his next words. She stared at him with so much hatred and disgust that it nearly set her on fire. She spoke slow and deliberate. "Father, I want you to arrange for my journey to take place as of tomorrow. Please and thank you."

She made her way to the door, but glanced over her shoulder when he said, "You are the best shepherdess I have and the accounting of books will be delayed. I can't replace you. The request is denied."

Rachel glared at her father one last time, before going to her room to pack her things. "What I'm asking you to do shouldn't be too difficult. Look how well you arranged this deceitful escapade. Make it happen, father. And that's my final request."

Laban decided not to say another word. He did not want to chance another scene, only minutes before the wedding ceremony. Since her grandparents had already arrived for the wedding, he would speak to Adinah's parents and see to it that his daughter was on her way to their home at daybreak. He could at least do that. Though he would feel her absence in his bank accounts. For anyone asking why this particular daughter was away, it would easily be explained away with two words—wedding planning.

As promised, Rachel returned to her rooms at the far end of the house. She could faintly hear the music announcing the ceremonies were about to begin. She had already begun to pack, but somehow found her knees weakening from the despair that filled her body. She fell across her bed. The torrent started with one tear, then, like a flood gate, her body was wracked with inconsolable sobs. The pain was unbearable, but she reminded herself it's only for a season. Her turn was coming. She would have her revenge, but most of all, she would have her Jacob.

CHAPTER 19

L eah stared at her gorgeous reflection in the mirror and smiled. She was dressed in the gown originally created for Rachel. Though she didn't choose the design, it was absolutely stunning. Especially on her. Alterations were easy, as their mother was skilled in this particular art. The key attribute was the veil. Here is where extra attention was given so that the layers of the veil fell heavy in the right areas around the face. No one would know she wasn't Rachel.

She was grateful that, as tradition would have it, there was no unveiling at the altar for the groom to kiss the bride. All physical touching would take place in the privacy of the honeymoon suite, a special cottage on the property prepared for the couple to steal away to enjoy their wedding night.

Leah had a quick moment where she felt sorry for Rachel—but that sentiment immediately evaporated when the words her sister had thrown out came flooding back. *Let me tell you. You aren't woman enough for Jacob—you ugly slant-eyed heifer. You may have won round one, but know this, Leah, in the end, I will win.*

She stood in front of the full-length mirror and appraised the intricate design of the floor-length white linen gown. The sleeves of her dress were sprinkled with diamond studs, starting from her wrist and connecting at the shoulder, with delicate white buttons that went all the way down her back. She felt like a princess and smiled as she whirled and twirled about the room. She was ready to marry her man.

* * *

Thirty minutes later, she thought she would die from the exhausting heat and the heaviness of that veil.

"Good grief! If ya'll keep this up, I'll faint while walking down the aisle. Give it a break for Pete's sake!" Leah jerked away from the group that surrounded her. "The way this thing hangs, even my mother and father will wonder whether it's me or Rachel."

One of the handmaids chuckled softly at that comment. Leah tried to turn and give the red-haired woman a warning glance but the material on her head shifted and she had to readjust quickly before the veil, with its long trail, fell.

A low scream from the pit of her stomach pushed its way out of her dry throat. "Fix this! Do you hear me! Tack this thing down so I can do a somersault and it'll still be in place. If that man sees my face before I become his wife, somebody in here is going to pay."

The handmaids quietly returned to ensuring Leah's outfit was properly fit. No one dared say a word. The light-hearted air of the room changed to a tense heaviness, full of anxiety on the part of the helpers. They loved Rachel, who had a more compassionate nature, a whole lot more than Leah.

Adinah heard the commotion outside her daughter's room. She never thought a wedding day could be so depressing. No matter where she went in the upper rooms, an air of apprehension or despair existed. She and Laban had convinced the immediate family that all the tension was normal for their household.

"We live in high anxiety all the time around here," she said to Laban's parents. "We are such perfectionists, you see. Once the ceremony begins, however, things will calm down and we can relax and enjoy the festivities."

Waiting for a signal that the shouting had died down, Adinah prepared to enter her oldest daughter's room to finalize the details of the deception. Laban, leaving the family's quarters, passed her in the hall. He paused to acknowledge her presence. She reached for his hand, and squeezed it tight.

"Laban, I pray our first born will marry and live happily with her husband," she said, then frowned as reality set in. "Well, at least she will fulfill the tradition and have a husband before her younger sister. I will leave the happy part in God's hands."

Jacob was more than a little surprised when Laban told him that Rachel wanted a more intimate wedding—only family and a few friends—but was actually relieved, as the pomp and circumstance of wedding ceremonial rituals was not a high priority for him. He was looking forward to the end of these ceremonies, and having Rachel all to himself. His loins were warmed at the thought.

Rachel had enough family in the area to achieve a lively celebration after the ceremony. As it stood, Jacob's parents would not be able to attend. Isaac, his father, was aged and blind, and his mother would not leave him for such a journey. He certainly knew his brother wasn't participating. Still a little upset about that whole stolen birthright thing. Man, could his brother hold a grudge.

With the ceremony about to begin, Jacob stood relaxed. He was impressed with how well the arrangements were going. Jacob and his best man were standing to the left of the chuppah, the ceremonial archway, with the Rabbi centered underneath. With the processional concluding, all brides' maids and groomsmen were in place.

Waiting for his soon to be wife, Jacob noticed the frantic activity in the aisle. Handmaids accidentally dropped a pile of lilies and red rose petals on the long white runner draped on the aisle, and were clearing the clutter before the bride appeared. Jacob was momentarily distracted, until he noticed the appearance of his bride. The parents' stood near their daughter, motionless, waiting. The organ played, as the bride entered. Jacob smiled while whispering, *Finally, my Rachel will be mine.*

The processional moved smoothly. Everyone was in place, and the timing perfect. In spite of the heavy veil, Leah was able to watch most of the activities from the side room. Now it was her turn. With her parents by her side, Leah began her walk toward her future.

"I can't breathe. I told them this was too much material," she mumbled.

"Quiet," Adinah snapped. "This is the price you pay to have what you want."

"You could've just told him what was up," she countered. "He probably would have gone for it."

"Are you sure you wanted to take the chance?" Laban shot back, putting a tighter grip on her upper hand. "Let's take off that veil right now and put it to the test, shall we?"

Leah's steps faltered and her head whipped toward Adinah, whose left eyebrow winged upward as if to say, *well?*

She resumed her walk down the aisle with her parents. She could barely see Jacob, but what she did take in took her breath away. He was strikingly handsome, dressed in a short white linen robe draped over his white shirt and pants, and he was smiling at her. She shifted a little with the anticipation of it all. "Ouch," she cried. "Something is sticking in my back. Mom, can you reach it?"

Adinah slowed the pace while smiling at the audience to put them at ease. "Let me check, baby. Just stay focused and keep walking." She slowly rubbed Leah's back, searching for any strange object that might be sticking through her dress. It wasn't easy because of the thickness of the veil.

Leah followed her mother's lead and slowed her pace, all while clenching her teeth. "If one of Rachel's crappy handmaids, ones that *you* decided should help, put something in this dress, I promise they will pay dearly for this prank."

Just as Leah finished her statement, those sudden pinches disappeared. They were still walking slowly down the aisle. "It's alright, mom. Whatever it was has stopped. Let's get this walk over with. Please, both of you smile. You look like you're going to prison."

That night, according to Hebrew tradition and Laban's plan, Jacob and Leah were married. Though not with as large a guest list as planned, everyone present was ready to party. And party is exactly what they did. There must have been one-hundred toasts to the couple, each one more tantalizing than the other. Leah picked up the glass, turned to face her mother, seated at the table, smiled, and waved in a salute. "I am so very happy mother, and it's all because of you." Just as Leah took her first sip, several drunken guests began shouting in Hebrew "Hi Lia (she is Leah)." The laughter grew louder and louder as others joined in.

Leah dropped her glass and turned to check Jacob's response. Jacob was so drunk; he didn't appear to hear or understand what was being said. She canvassed the room, searching for her father, and saw him standing near one of the lighted torches at the entrance to the room. Frantic, Leah waved for him to join her at the wedding table. With clinched teeth, she faced her mother.

"Can you believe this!" Leah was almost screaming. "Do you hear that! They're shouting my name." She stood, leaned across the table and grabbed her mother's hand. "Rachel is behind this. I know it, and you do too."

Adinah shifted uncomfortably. "Leah. Stop it," she whispered. You are drawing attention to yourself, and while getting upset for nothing." She yanked her hand from Leah and smoothed her hair. "Look at your husband. He's heard nothing."

Leah turned and observed. Jacob was swinging one arm, while drinking wine and cheering, oblivious to the commotion going on around him.

Laban was across the room, directing the servants to reduce the number of torches surrounding the celebration, to ensure room dim lighting. Having heard Leah's name being shouted, he waved to acknowledge his daughter's request to come to her. He moved through the crowd, continuing to shake hands, laugh, and cheer loudly, to distract from what was being said.

Laban reached the wedding table. He grabbed his wife's shoulders firmly. "Look up and smile," he whispered. "Wave to our guest, and act like I just asked you to dance." Adinah looked in her husband's eyes. "Get up now," Laban ordered, while tightening his grip on her shoulder.

Leah's mother lifted her head and smiled. She took her husband's hand as they moved to the dance floor. Laughing, Laban whirled his wife around the floor to the cheers of the drunken crowd. All attention had refocused on the parents of the bride. Emergency over. Secret secure. When the music ended, Laban and Adinah returned to the bridal table. Once seated, Adinah scowled at her husband through clinched teeth.

"You created this mess. Always planning and scheming, and somehow dragging me in when it gets too hot for you to handle. Well, my husband, hear this. I don't care if Rachel walks in this room right now, I am through with this circus." Laban leaned in to respond, but Adinah turned her head and began talking to one of the other guests. To ensure her dismissal of him didn't appear awkward to their guest, Laban laughed aloud, as if she said something funny, and then walked into the crowd.

Leah continued greeting well-wishers, while monitoring her husband's behavior. As the evening progressed, Leah felt Jacob fondling her leg and reaching for her face, signaling he was eager to unveil his bride. Leah fidgeted, removed his hand, and shook her head.

Adinah, noticing the tug of war, interceded. "Jacob, my son, remember our ritual dictates that you cannot unveil my daughter until in bridal chamber." He nodded, drank, laughed.

Rising from his chair, Jacob bowed. "You are correct mother. I look forward to the moment." He smiled at his bride. "I'm going to dance for you, my sweet." Jacob stumbled over a chair while going to the dance floor. The crowd laughed and cheered while Jacob whirled around the floor with his buddies in drunken stupor.

* * *

Leah left the celebration just as Jacob's buddies were pouring several cups of coffee into their friend. Now she waited for him in their wedding chamber. Only one candle was lit, sitting on the dressing table in the far corner of the room. The canopy bed had been draped in champagne-colored silk and covered with soft blue dyed lace trimmed in diamond studs that sparkled from the flickering of the candlelight. Leah was in a silk negligee. She sat in the corner of the bed, waiting in the shadows of the curtain.

As she waited, Leah heard Jacob and his friends singing loud, and off-key on the grounds. They were guiding him toward their honeymoon cottage, shouting good wishes. After a few moments, their voices trailed to a distance as they walked away.

Leah decided to confess who she was as soon as Jacob entered the room. The deceit had gone far enough and she decided he could handle it at that point. She was first born and had to marry first. He would understand, right? In the middle of her thoughts, the bedroom door opened and Jacob stumbled inside the room.

"Alright, thanks, you guys." Jacob entered the room, waving to them. Barely able to stand, he began shedding his clothes. The sight of his abs, well-defined muscle, the whole picture of him left her speechless. He climbed into bed whispering, "Rachel, my Rachel."

Before Leah could respond, his mouth covered hers and nothing else mattered. She loved Jacob so much—from day one she wanted him. Their lovemaking was full of more passion than Leah could have ever imagined. That night the deception was complete. There was no turning back now. By law and tradition, Leah was his wife.

CHAPTER 20

Jacob's voice shook the rafters the next morning as he roared, "What in the entire—"

Eyes wide with shock, he yanked the covers off Leah. "What are you doing here? Where is Rachel?"

Leah reached for Jacob's. "You're married to me. Everything will be explained. Please be patient. I love you." She smiled and touched his arm. With her virtue missing in action, the first Mrs. Jacob had firmly secured her position. Whether he liked it or not. And he didn't like it one bit.

Jacob was shocked, furious, and distraught at the trick that had been played on him. He pushed Leah aside, got out of bed, and grabbed his pants. "I can't believe this. Where is Rachel? Where is your father? Get dressed, Leah. Don't say another word. Just get dressed." Jacob slammed the door and left Leah in tears.

After a few minutes searching, he found Laban in his study, busy with paperwork, and issuing orders to several of his workmen. He was back to operating business as usual. Jacob stood at the threshold. "Laban, we have to talk. I need to speak to you *right now* and in private."

Laban frowned, then dismissed his servants, and closed the study door. Before he could speak, Jacob approached this man who seemed more like a stranger to him now.

"What have you done to me, man? We had a deal. You promised me Rachel's hand in marriage for the seven years I served as the manager of your business and properties."

He punched a fist into his palm as he continued. "I worked hard, made you good money, never complained even when I knew you were skimming some of the profits off the top, and off the books, to make sure you didn't have to pay higher taxes. You made a fool out of me. I want some answers. And where is Rachel?"

Laban moved toward Jacob, using slow deliberate steps. "Son, please sit down and let me talk to you. When you hear what I have to say, you will understand why you had to marry Leah, and you will be pleased to learn you can have Rachel too ... *in due time*."

"In due time," Jacob snapped. "What the ... what is that supposed to mean?"

His father-in-law took a deep breath, as though he was the one who needed to be calm. "You see, there are customs here that we must follow. It is just not done here in our country that the youngest be married before the firstborn. It would be an affront to tradition, but I do have a proposition for you."

Laban slid another agreement in Jacob's direction. "If you stay with me and be a husband to Leah for a little while, Rachel can also be your wife."

Jacob sat in the chair his father-in-law always offered business associates. He rubbed his goatee, as he studied his father-in-law's- tired round face, looking for an emotion he could read. A lot of good that would do since he missed the mark on this whole bride-swap deal. Having worked for Laban for years, he had many opportunities to observe how the man operated. "Work for you a little while longer, huh? How long is *a little while*, Laban?"

Laban moved closer to Jacob, smiling to relax the atmosphere. "Let's say you work for me another seven years. At the end of seven years, you Rachel, and Leah leave and go live where you choose."

Jacob jumped from his seat. Now he was beyond anger and heading fast to outright rage. "Another seven years!? What kind of fool do you take me for? How do you expect me to live with a woman I don't love?" Then his gaze narrowed on the man who was taking way too much satisfaction in this unfortunate turn of events. "And why seven years?"

Laban tapped his desk chair while observing Jacob, as he paced back and forth in front of him like a caged animal.

"Jacob," he said as he stood and leaned forward to ensure the young man was paying attention. "Seven years is the time period I ask you to commit to me as your gift before you can start a new life with Rachel and Leah. But of course, I certainly wouldn't have you delay marrying Rachel for such a length of time. I only ask that you agree to wait one week before that ceremony takes place. This is a reasonable length of time to satisfy the gossip, don't you think Jacob? We don't want it to appear that you *had* to marry Leah."

Laban walked around his desk and approached Jacob again, arms open. The smile had returned to his face.

"I have already spoken to Rachel. She is willing, my son. It's just one week. By waiting this short time, your marriage to her would not be a strain on the family. On the contrary, it would be most acceptable. Just think, is this really too much to ask? Especially since you love her so much."

Rachel knew about this and didn't say a word? No wonder she never responded to the notes I sent her during that day. She knew.

She knew!

Jacob pushed from Laban's grip and backed away. He opened the office door, prepared to leave. In spite of the tacky way he was treated, he was still in love with Rachel.

"I'll agree to these terms, Laban, and work the additional seven years. Apparently, there's no other way out of this mess. I'll go tell Rachel."

Laban returned to his desk. "Well, that's the one other thing I wanted to tell you. Rachel isn't here. She's has chosen to visit with her grandparents for the days leading up to your ceremony, as part of the arrangement to further dispel any potential gossip. Don't worry, she'll return within six days. This is for the best, my son."

Jacob glared at his father-in-law. "What treachery. You really worked this scheme to the fullest, didn't you?" He slammed the door and left.

Jacob couldn't believe the old man had the nerve to try to smooth the whole situation over with a corny crack about how "this is for the best, my son."

No one believed it.

Adinah arose early to see Rachel off to visit with the grandparents. Entering the room she saw her giddy, almost gliding around, with a satchel, finalizing the packing. Before leaving, Rachel provided details of her meeting with Laban, including having to wait only one week before marrying Jacob. "So, you see mother, your precious Leah didn't win after all. Actually, she whispered, from what I hear she was almost discovered during the celebration last night."

Adinah stiffened, eyebrows tight. "Rachel, I warn you. Your disrespectful tone will no longer be tolerated. We did have one or two mishaps last evening. I just hope you had nothing to do with it." She approached her daughter with a tight-lipped smile. "Okay. So good. You will marry your Jacob in a week. Your father told me the news this morning. I hope this resolves the issues, and we can begin to return to some normalcy in this family."

Rachel grunted, gave her mother a deep bow, and walked to the door. She paused and tilted her head, while giving a dismissive wave. "I will see you soon, mother." Closing the door, she breathed deep, and left to join the caravan for her trip.

Adinah breathed heavy and walked toward the wedding cottage. She knew her husband was meeting with Jacob at this moment. In fact, it seems to entire household knew Jacob was meeting with her husband. No matter where she walked, there was muffled giggles then silence when she appeared. The turmoil and upheaval in her home was no a secret to anyone for miles around. She was sure of it. As she approached the cottage, sounds of voices floated from the pathway ahead. Several handmaids were in a cluster laughing and talking. They were coming from the direction of the cottage.

"Girl, he was shouting for her to shut up and get away from him," one of the handmaids said, as she giggled. "Then he stormed out of that place. She was wailing up a storm." Slapping her hand on her thigh, the maid smirked. "What a mess."

Adinah coughed. The women jumped, looking at each other sheepishly. Stepping between them, Adinah stared at each other as if to remember their faces. All the handmaids bowed and kept their eyes to the ground.

"You have work to do, don't you?" Scanning the group, each handmaid nodded in agreement. "Then do it, Adinah shouted." Everyone scurried in different directions.

Adinah approached and knocked gently on the cottage door then called to her daughter. No answer. She opened the door. Leah was sitting in the corner of the bed, eyes bloodshot, puffing and panting as if she was unable to catch her breath. Adinah walked to the bed, and sat near her daughter. Touching her face, she waited for Leah's breathing to become normal.

"We had a crisis and it's over."

Leah, glared at her mother. "We?" She sniffed. "We had a crisis?" She scowled. "My husband hates me and will probably never touch me again, and we had a crisis that's over."

Adinah moved closer to her daughter. The next bit of information would be biting for Leah but must be said.

"Leah, you had to know Jacob would be shocked and upset to learn he didn't marry the person promised to him. That cannot be a surprise to you. But it is done. He is meeting with your father now about the new arrangements, and everything will be fine."

Leah shifted away from her mother, curled her knees to her chin and spoke in a low almost inaudible voice. "What do you mean new arrangements? What has father done now?"

Adinah stood and began to pace. Leah watched in silence. Adinah shared the news. "Rachel has left, you know that. What you don't know is plans have changed for the second wedding between your sister and Jacob. Instead of it taking place in seven years, it will take place in one week. She will visit with your grandparents, to allow you time as a newlywed, and return in time for her marriage ceremony, a week from now."

Leah threw herself full on the bed and began to scream and cry. "That heifer, that scrawny, too cute for herself bag of camel dung. You let her win! You let her win! I have no time to change his mind, to help him see me as the better one. You and father ruined my life."

Adinah grabbed her daughter's shoulders firmly. "Look at me. You wanted Jacob, you got him. If you are smart, you will make the best of these six days alone with him. He will return soon. Wash your body and put on your prettiest attire. Make it work, Leah. You have no other choice." With that final remark, Adinah wiped her daughter's face, hugged, and left the wedding cottage. She had performed her task. The rest was up to her daughter.

After meeting with Laban, Jacob returned to face Leah, but he couldn't bear to look at her. He had always spurned her advances, knowing his heart was firmly in Rachel's hands. This was one heck of a way to begin a marriage. Everyone, including his Rachel, joined in this deception. But he wasn't one to talk. Especially with what he had done to his brother, Esau. Looks like that whole reap what you sow is a reality.

Tensions were a little high for several days, but Jacob finally settled down and adjusted to a life with his "first" wife, while looking forward to gaining the right to marry the love of his life.

CHAPTER 21

Rachel opened her eyes. For a moment she thought she was back in Bethel, with her grandparents. She blinked twice, trying to clear the cobwebs of thought from her mind. Yep, she was home. Definitely a far cry from the beautiful mountains and vegetation of Judah, and frequent opportunities to visit the rivers of the Jordan while shopping. Rising, she plumped the large pillows to brace her back. Covering her face, she wept. The heartbreak hit her all over again. Leah was sleeping with her man.

Rachel had arrived home from her six-day hiatus right before supper. The house had been quiet. The handmaids she had left behind, since she had only been allowed to take one, had eagerly greeted her at the door upon her arrival. Their eyes and smiling faces had been a welcomed sight.

Rachel's room was in the west wing of her father's spacious home, so there was little chance she would see anyone else unless they had been informed of her arrival. By the looks of the few people who greeted her last night, no one else was made aware when she would come home. Rachel breathed a sigh of relief, as she got out of bed and approached the balcony door. She was in no mood for a welcome home celebration or small talk. She already had enough going on with having to plan a wedding. The scenery was as beautiful as she remembered, and provided the calm she needed before starting the day.

As she stepped back inside and, to her surprise, was greeted by her mother. Adinah hugged her daughter for a long time.

"Welcome home, baby girl. It's so good to see you. We have everything ready and waiting for you to review in preparation for your wedding ceremony. We've also shifted some things around so the entire four rooms of the west wing are now dedicated to you and your handmaids, including your two former handmaids. Everything is as you left it. Just waiting for your return."

Rachel was happy to see her mother, but didn't particularly want to hear about or take a grand tour of her new settings. She was sure they were created to keep as much distance between her, Jacob, and Leah as possible, and to ensure a peaceful existence among the family. She hugged her mom briefly, yawned, and stretched dramatically, then started to walk toward her bath area.

"Thank you, mom. It's been a long journey, and I'm still tired. I feel like crap right now, and need a bath. Actually, I think I could sleep for a full day."

Adinah knew her daughter enough to recognize she was still steaming behind the situation between Leah and Jacob. The bitter tint of her tone signaled it was painfully clear this was going to be an awkward transition. When Rachel arrived late the evening before, Laban had chickened out and made the last-minute decision to greet his daughter at breakfast.

Adinah walked quickly in the direction of the bedroom door. "We thought that would be the case, so I'm having a fruit, cheese, broth and bread platter sent to your room." She glanced over her shoulder leaving the suite. "You get some rest, and I will see you later today."

* * *

After her bath, Rachel went back to bed. She scanned the room. Her bed was in front of windows overlooking the vast greenery of her father's property. The sun beamed bright, bringing a warmth she didn't feel. Sun lint—what they used to call the specs of dust in the atmosphere that could only be seen from the sunbeams coming through the windows—danced on the beams. Rachel drifted to sleep and dreamed of the fun times she and Leah used to have as children trying to catch the lint particles. Of course, the dream ended with Leah complaining to her mother because she thought Rachel caught more of them than she had.

It was mid-afternoon when Rachel heard a knock then her room door opened. One of her handmaids entered with a tray of sliced lamb, mixed vegetable, grapes and honey buns. She was followed by her mother carrying a flask of water and cups.

"Since we weren't sure if you were up to joining us for lunch this afternoon, thought I'd have this meal prepared for you," she said while spreading the meal on a nearby table. "Of course, if you'd rather come down and have lunch with the rest of us, I can have this tray sent back to the kitchen. I just wasn't sure what you preferred."

Rachel remained quiet while observing her mother. Adinah had been a key player in issues surrounding planning Jacob and Leah's wedding. Rachel knew she was a daddy's girl, because of her excellent competence as shepherdess. That fact, however, didn't keep him from throwing her under the bus, when the money Jacob represented was on the table.

"Thank you, mom. I appreciate your thoughtfulness. I should be down later today."

Walking to the door, Adinah paused and smiled. "It really is good to have you home again." Rachel shrugged, but didn't respond. Adinah sighed opened the door and left.

Rachel knew her actions from now on would set the tone of her relationship with Jacob, but she still needed some time before joining the family gathering. She feared he was now going to give her the side-eye, cool reception because, he believed had been part of a scheme from the beginning. Laban had put her in a situation where she couldn't have her beloved unless she betrayed his trust. Not the best position for a woman to be in. *Would Jacob ever trust her again?*

* * *

Rachel spent the rest of the afternoon meeting with her assigned attendants, directing the details of the decorations needed in place for the ceremony. With all instructions issued, and everyone sent to various assignments, only her private handmaid remained to finish unpacking. Rachel strolled onto her balcony.

Scanning the area, she noticed the plants had been well attended. Her favorites, the lilies, were in full bloom. She peered over the edge and noticed, beyond the clearing of trees below, their pool seating arrangements had been finalized. Then she saw him. Jacob was walking through the garden toward the main house. He was having a conversation with one of the attendants. She started to get his attention, but hesitated. Before she could change her mind, he was out of view. Smiling, Rachel returned to her bedroom and saw Leah standing in the doorway.

"Welcome home sister Ray," Leah shouted. She enjoyed watching Rachel frown, knowing she hated that nickname. Leah folded her arms and leaned against the doorframe.

"Enjoying the view of decorations for your ceremony planned tomorrow?" Walking to the side table, Leah grabbed a fig and tossed it in the air. "I hope the plans meet with your approval. You certainly have them hopping around here. as you prepare to become the second wife."

Running fingers through her hair then tossing it back over her shoulders, Leah moved closer to her sister and smiled. "I already had full pleasure of his body, my dear, and it was good," she sneered.

Rachel walked toward her sister, fist clinched, eyes piercing Leah's gaze with such hate she stepped back. She stood so close to her sister, their noses almost touch.

"You pitiful excuse for a woman. You think because you have sex with the man you tricked into marrying that you have gained the love, bonding, and connection afforded a real covenant?" She shouted. "Not so you crossed eyed ninny. You have fooled no one. In fact, I hear the guest were even laughing and calling your name at the reception last week."

Rachel tugged Leah's blouse collar. "Jacob's heart belongs to me and tomorrow so will his body. He will perform husbandry duties with you, Leah, but he will make love to me. Now, be the snake that you are and slither out of my room. You stench the air with you scent of deceit. Go! Enjoy you day and night, for tomorrow Jacob will marry the love of his life, and you will be put in your place behind me."

Leah was speechless for a moment. "Well, my dear, it appears you are a bit frazzled. This is your room, and I will be happy to leave. I just wanted to give you the proper greeting, sister to sister, before our little gathering later. I see we understand each other perfectly."

Stepping back, she turned and moved to the door, as if a ballerina dancing, Pausing, she tossed a final comment.

"You think you have Jacob's love, but I have proven to you over and over again that I can always get things to work my way." Shoving the handmaid aside, Leah opened the bedroom door, threw her sister a kiss. "Welcome home," she smirked, and slammed the door.

Rachel stood still, for a moment, watching the door—almost expecting Leah to open it again to offer another comment. Turning her attention from the door, she pointed to the remaining travel bag. "Let's leave this one closed for the moment. I will handle it myself." She grabbed her prettiest dress and threw it on the bed.

Searching for sandals, she instructed her handmaid, "prepare my bath." The handmaid nodded, bowed, and left the room. Frustrated that she allowed Leah to instigate a fight, Rachel decided it was time to join the family group. The sun was high, just before setting. Its beams streamed through the shear curtains creating a soft glow. The soft breeze added to the quiet atmosphere of her room. With a sigh of relief, she leaned against the opening. It was once again quiet and beautiful.

"Hey Kiddo," Aunt Sylvia chided softly peeping in the bedroom. "It's almost time for dinner and you've been up here the whole day. Are you coming out to play?"

"Yep," Rachel laugh, I'm almost ready." Just finished my bath," she responded while reaching for her robe and sandals.

Her aunt stepped inside and sat on one of the cushion chairs. "Good, its's time to make your presence known."

Rachel loved Aunt Sylvia. She had been widowed several years ago, but hadn't let the loss prevent her from living a full life. She retired from managing the vineyards of her husband's estate, established a circle of friends, and spent most of the time traveling and writing. Though her mother's sister, they had very little in common. Her aunt was independent and self-sufficient.

Always busy, Sylvia moved the canvas bags blocking the closet doors, so she could hang a sheath dress Rachel had thrown on a chair. "What's this?" Aunt Sylvia asked as she pulled a picture from behind the lounge chair.

"Oh that." Rachel smiled, moved slightly, then stretched. "It's a picture of a mandrake plant."

Aunt Sylvia laughed, peering at the drawing. "A what?"

Rachel paused while dressing, and smiled at her aunt. "A mandrake plant," she repeated. "They grow in the Mediterranean," Rachel explained while pointing to the picture. "This picture of the mandrake was painted by an artist I met. I bought it to remind me of my trip." *And as an insurance policy for my future, if the need arises.* "It's been said that this plant aids in fertility."

Aunt Sylvia stared at the painting, turning it around several directions. "Uh, okay. Well come on, kiddo. Let's decide what you're wearing. Don't forget it's your homecoming celebration tonight."

Rachel laughed. "That's right," she said with a hint of excitement. "Tonight, we celebrate my homecoming. Tomorrow we celebrate my wedding."

"I'll fix that pompous dung head," Leah mumbled while leaving the suite of rooms she shared with Jacob on her way downstairs. Several handmaids passed her quickly loaded with what appeared to be supplies needed for the outdoor decorations. With her mother twisting her arm, she reluctantly agreed for them to gather some materials stored in the cabinets in her suite "It's always about her," she mumbled.

Leah reached the bottom in time for Adinah, to say, "Hey! Perfect timing. I was just about to check on your sister. It's about time for her to get up. Her friends should be here soon and I don't want to get stuck entertaining them while she's getting dressed." She gestured to a point behind her. "Can you go check on her for me?"

Leah sighed heavily, not looking forward to laying eyes on the woman who still had Jacob's heart. "Look, Mom, I'm sure she's being well cared for right now. Aunt Sylvia is pampering her at the moment. I have no doubt she'll be ready on time. Besides, I'm in no mood to play servant to her needs today." Then she smiled. "Remember, I have a husband to take care of, in spite how people are trying to forget I ever had a wedding."

Adinah shook her head as she watched Leah saunter towards the kitchen. "I had fresh salad prepared and chicken, lamb, and carp fillets smoking in the pit," she shouted while heading toward her bedroom suite. "Please make sure the staff pulls out the platters of dates, nut bread, and mixed fresh vegetables. We'll all be down in a minute for a quick meal to catch up with things and firm up the wedding plans."

Leah kept walking, acting as if she didn't hear a word her mother said. She had her own set of problems, and her sister coming home to be with Jacob was the major one.

That spoiled little heifer hadn't been out of the picture long enough to suit Leah's taste. even days had passed, and Leah couldn't win Jacob over. The marriage had been so much more tense than she'd expected. No real love, no real affection. Jacob didn't fall in love with her as she had hoped. Barely touched her since the wedding night, no matter what tricks she tried. This made her even more desperate to get pregnant as soon as possible.

To add insult to injury, she now had to watch while Rachel becomes Jacob's bride. In fact, daddy's girl was back and Leah had seen neither hide nor hair of Jacob all morning. *Why hang around the substitute when the real thing had arrived?* All the work she'd put into their marriage this last week, and now she was no more than a convenient, live-in caretaker. One thing was certain, when this wedding was over, she'd have to figure out what life was going to be like with Rachel all up in the mix.

CHAPTER 22

Wine glass in hand, Sylvia shouted from the hallway. "Alright, ladies, dinner is on the table. Let's eat." Adinah laughed and shook her head as she joined her sister to help escort the last two family members to the welcome celebration gathering. Everyone else was already seated, drinking and talking.

Leah dragged herself from the couch in her mother's sitting area and Rachel came bounding down the stairs, two steps at a time. They met halfway in the hall, eyeing each other like two bulls ready to charge.

"Hey, what are you doing?" Rachel said. "That's my shawl. Where did you get that?"

"From your bag," Leah answered, staring at Rachel with contempt.

"I figured you wouldn't mind since you came home with a boat load of new clothes." She smoothed her hand slowly down the expensive high neck, white wool material trimmed in silver beads. "Besides, this style looks much better on me, don't you think?"

"I don't care how you look," Rachel snapped as she moved toward her sister. "I didn't give you permission to borrow my clothes. Take it off."

Hearing the noise, their mother rushed into the hallway. "Girls, what's the problem?"

Rachel turned to face the woman who had always favored Leah over her. "The problem is your daughter **is** wearing my clothes without my permission."

Leah sneered at her sister. "My goodness, I just borrowed it for tonight's *celebration*." "What's the beef? You have loads of shawls. I just wanted to look nice for *your* event, so I picked one. This one."

Leah smiled, brushed past them and continued moving toward the dining room where the family awaited. Before she took her next few steps, Rachel yanked her sister's arm and squeezed hard. "OK, Leah. Game's up" She whispered through clinched teeth. "You've spent a lifetime making excuses as to why you did something that suited you, no matter who it affected. Your tricks and the shabby way you got married last week, is the ultimate last straw. Do you hear me? It stops today." Rachel relaxed her grip, but still held her sister's arm. "So here are your choices. You ask me, right now, if you can wear my shawl or you take your rear end upstairs and take it off."

Adinah moved quickly to step between the two sisters. She turned her head, and looked at Rachel who ignored the look. "I'm waiting Leah, she said firmly."

Leah chuckled. "All this over nothing. So, OK." She pushed her sister's hand to release the grip. With her hands clasped in prayer fashion, she bowed and asked permission using a sweet, slurpy tone. "Ms. Rachel, she said with a over sweet voice. "May I please wear your shawl this evening?"

Adinah rubbed her daughter's arm. "See, she asked permission." Rachel glared at her mother, then looked directly in her sister's eyes. "Make this the last time you take anything of mine." Leah smiled, adjusted the shawl and sauntered toward the dining area. She gave

Rachel one last look before entering. "I don't need anything else of yours, sis. Jacob is quite enough for me."

It doesn't seem to matter what that girl does," Rachel said to her mother, while pulling her into the pantry to hold a private conversation. Aunt Sylvia following.

"You always find a reason to excuse her behavior, and it always leads with her "condition." She's twenty-six years old, and you've made her an emotional cripple. And she loves it."

Adinah was taken aback by her daughter's words and the tone. "Rachel, I love you both. I admit, because of her condition, Leah may have demanded more of my attention through the years. Though she's the oldest sibling, you are the strongest. I never worry that you are able to make it on your own if I am not here to help."

Rachel paced the floor, silent. Adinah approached cautiously and touched her daughter's face gently. "You were allowed to go away because your father and I knew you would take the time to adjust, regroup, and return ready to make the best of the situation. Come on, baby girl. Show us we weren't wrong."

Rachel raised both hands in the air, shrugged then hugged her mother. "Ok, mother. Issue resolved. I'm good. Let's get this gathering over with. I want to get ready for my wedding tomorrow."

While embracing her daughter, Adinah noticed Sylvia standing in the doorway of the pantry, eyeing her with such disdain. Stepping back from their embrace, Adinah smiled and pointed at her sister. "Look at that woman over there with a glass of wine and none for us. Let's go catch up." Everyone laughed.

Following her sister and niece toward the dining area, Sylvia tugged

Adinah's arm. "Got a minute Sis? I want to talk to you about our special surprise for this young lady tomorrow morning."

Smiling, Sylvia faced her niece. "Rachel you go ahead and get seated, I just want to make sure your mom and I have this treat ready." Rachel hugged them both and entered the dining room.

Sylvia and Adinah returned to the privacy of the pantry. Sylvia sipped her wine while adjusting her position next to the food counter. "After observing yet another frigid moment between my nieces, with the piercing looks that could slice ice, I think you guys need to address the situation before it gets way out of hand. Conversation between them was minimal to none during the best of times. Now, with this marriage stuff, reconciliation without intercession seems impossible."

Adinah listened to her sister ramble on and on about how bad things are between Leah and Rachel, then interrupted. She pushed the pantry door closed and raised her hand. "Sylvia, stop. I know my daughters. Given time, things will be back to normal with them. It's only a matter of being patient and letting the dust settle."

Sylvia placed her wine glass on a cloth lying on the counter, and smoothed the edges. Rubbing her hands together, she looked directly at her sister. "Adinah, you're living in la la land." These girls have little or no interest in reconciling. There's more to this than a disagreement over a blasted shawl, and somebody's got to help these girls figure out how they're going to share one husband between them."

She leaned forward to ensure her sister was listening. "You need to call a meeting, let them lay their thoughts on the table, so we can help resolve the issue. I don't believe in letting stuff fester. It solves nothing and creates more damage in the long run. So why don't you—"

Adinah raised her hand. "Enough. Enough! I don't need any more unsolicited opinions on what you think I should do. Leah and Rachel are my daughters, not yours. I'm sure you have good intentions, but you don't have full details about any of this situation. I neither have the time nor inclination to talk anymore with you about it."

Adinah breathed and reached for her sister's hand. "I know you mean well and I love you for it, but I know what's best for my girls. They know I'm here to listen and support them. There are two sides to every conversation, and I fully intend to hear both sides in due time. Right now, they're in a cooling down period which may seem a bit long for you, but I believe our patience will have its reward."

Sylvia drained her wine glass. "As you wish, I will back off, but something is very wrong and—" Adinah raised one hand, and walked to the pantry exit.

Talking to her back, Sylvia continued. "I'm just saying, we're sitting on top of an emotional powder keg. But I promise I won't say another word."

Adinah stopped in the doorway and looked back. "Thank you, Sis. Come on, let's eat." Sylvia laughed. "You eat. I'm getting another glass of wine."

Several hours had passed since the welcome home celebration for Rachel. During the event, communication between the two sisters was limited to one or two words—yes, no, excuse me, and good night.

Leah didn't seem to care about the tension with her sister. She was determined to create dissension and unrest in the household, especially since Rachel's wedding would outshine Leah's by far—in the number of invited guests, and in the fact that Jacob would be marrying the woman he loved. The man was practically walking on air. So of course, Leah was taking it out on Rachel. And there wasn't much anyone could do about it.

The wedding was the most extravagant celebration many of the guests had ever seen. Unbeknownst to her parents, while away, Rachel pulled together resources, with her grandparents and close friends helping, in advance of her return, so that decorations arrived by caravan very early the day of the ceremony. All hands-on deck, every able-bodied member of the household worked diligently to ensure the garden area was transformed into an elegant scene.

Jacob and Rachel's marital covenant took place in the cool of the evening, as the sun set over the horizon. Rachel's veil was deliberately thin, a subtle slap at Leah, and her dress was designed to complement her body.

The wedding celebration lasted long into the night, with Rachel going to the wedding chambers well after midnight to prepare to greet her husband. Jacob drank much less wine this night. He wanted to consummate the marriage having full control of his faculties and enjoy every moment with her, creating a long-lasting memory. He finally had his true love, his Rachel.

* * *

Leah went to her quarters as soon as the wedding ceremony was over. In spite of how she knew it would feel, being present as Jacob entered the covenant with her sister was important.

It made the situation more real to her. Still determined she would earn Jacob's favor, Leah resolved to bear him a child as soon as possible, and demonstrate she was better suited to be his wife. He belonged to her and she to him. In time he would realize this. She would be patient. There was still time. Convinced things would work in her favor, Leah climbed into bed, covered her head with pillows, and tried to prevent her thoughts from drifting. It didn't work. She cried.

CHAPTER 23

Feeling nauseated, Leah entered the bathroom for the fifth time. At first, these bouts hit only in the mornings. Now her stomach stayed upset all day long. According to custom, despite all of the modern conveniences, she had gathered and urinated on the same small pile of wheat and barley seeds set aside for the test. She was to perform this function for several days. Today, she performed the seventh one. As the directions provided, if the wheat sprouted, she was having a girl. If the barley sprouted, she was having a boy. If neither sprouted, then she wasn't pregnant at all.

Leah looked carefully at the pile, then dropped down on the cushioned chair situated near the balcony. A broad smile began to slowly spread across her face. It's a girl. I'm giving my husband a seventh child, and it's a girl. She was happy. Seven children in seven years. "Let's see his precious Rachel beat that, she whispered. Heck, she got a long way to go."

When she tipped down the stairs, her mother and aunt were laughing on the upper deck. Leah paused. She simply wasn't in the mood for pretending. She needed help. She needed her mom.

Leah could smell the fresh roses from the bushes along the wall below the deck and could hear the water splashing as the workmen cleared some of the debris from the pool. This was her favorite place.

Aunt Sylvia narrowed a gaze on her and smirked before taking a sip of red wine. Leah's handmaids were attending the boys.

As she entered the deck area, her mom looked up, pleasantly surprised. "Hey honey, come on over."

Leah felt Aunt Sylvia studying her as she flopped down on one of the deck chairs. She'd scanned Leah in the same manner many times over the past few weeks, with the gaze always landing on her belly.

I guess she won't be surprised at my news.

"So, you finally decided to join us old ladies for some sun and fun, huh?"

Leah grabbed a piece of fruit "Not exactly, Mom. I need to talk to ya'll."

The knowing look Aunt Sylvia gave over the rim of her wineglass angered Leah to no end. Aunt Sylvia was such a know it all sometimes. Right or wrong, she knew it all.

"I could drag this out, but I can't think of a reason why." Feeling queasy, Leah dropped the half-eaten fruit on the table, then rubbed her stomach gently. "I'm pregnant."

She didn't know what to do with the silence that followed. Pregnancy was a good thing. Being fruitful, multiplying, and all that. They should have been jumping for joy.

Leah shifted in her chair uncomfortably and scanned the area. The birds were chirping. Bees were humming around the flowers in the planters near the pool. The soft breeze was blowing. Everything was normal except the tension in the air. Leah knew she had crushed her mom's perfect world—well, Rachel's perfect world— again. Each time

166

Leah is pregnant, the riff between them is magnified until the baby is born. As Leah taunts her sister with her condition Adinah spends months as referee, because Rachel is frustrated with her barren state.

First the marriage to Jacob, then she's the first one out of the gate to get pregnant, not once, but six times since her marriage. Now...batter up! Here she is about to announce her seventh child. All attention will return to taking care of depressed Rachel.

Leah decided to break the deadening silence, adjusting her chair as she forced a smile. "Sorry, mom. I had planned to tell you first before anyone else but couldn't seem to catch you alone lately," she explained as she cut her eyes over to her Aunt Sylvia.

Leah observed the scowl that remained on her mother's face. She turned to her Aunt Sylvia. "Auntie, I know you will respect my wishes and let everyone find out when Mom does a special announcement." Leah knew Aunt Sylvia was bound to tell Rachel, even if she couldn't count on her mother to tip that scale.

Her aunt smiled, then cut her eyes over to her sister, and nodded. "Besides, we want to keep this special moment unique and set apart from all the flurry around our moving plans." Leah was determined to have her baby celebration be so extravagant and unique, it would overshadow the upcoming farewell celebration Rachel planned for their move. In the meantime, she knew she had to play the announcement to the max. She inhaled, reached deep, and unleashed the waterworks.

With her tears flowing freely, Leah talked about how sick she'd been and how she felt she was going through this alone. Adinah pulled her chair closer, enveloping Leah in a hug. She sold her mother on the idea of treating this birth event like it was the first child because of the significance of the number seven in their faith. Leah put her head on Adinah's shoulder and they hugged tightly.

"Mom, this whole thing is so special because seven is the number of completion. It is a prime number." She placed a trembling hand on her belly. "This is my seventh child."

Leah paused to let her statement sink in a moment, but Aunt Sylvia rolled her eyes heavenward. *Tough old dove.*

"These facts are just too important to ignore. My pregnancy and child birthing event should be part of a major celebration," she said in a voice just above a whisper. "This is going to be a very special baby who will be loved by a very special grand mom." Leah and her mother began to laugh and cry at the same time.

The only other sound on the deck was Aunt Sylvia picking up the bottle of wine and pouring a tall drink for herself and a short glass of wine for her sister. She slid over another vessel to serve up a glass of orange juice for her niece.

Sylvia sat quietly drinking as the evening made its presence known, while the "Leah show" took center stage. Adinah and her daughter were heavy in baby celebration preliminary planning discussions. When Leah had exhausted the main topics and extracted that firm commitment from her mom for a huge celebration, there was a moment of silence as they sipped beverages and enjoyed to evening breeze.

The silence was interrupted by the sound of giddy laughter and the clatter of feet. "Mother! Mother!" Rachel burst in the room laughing with two of her handmaids following. When she saw the other members, Rachel paused. Scanning the room, she noticed the empty wine glasses. Leah shifted position on the cushions near her mother, but Adinah tapped Leah's shoulder and adjusted so she could stand to greet her daughter.

"What is it?! Are you alright?" Rachel smiled. "Mother, I am fine. In fact, I'm wonderful. I am pregnant! Best yet, according to the test, it's a boy, she laughed!" Leah, stared at her sister, but didn't speak.

Aunt Sylvia lifted her glass high in the air. "I just have one final comment for the evening." The other women's attention focused on her. "Congratulations to all," she said dryly.

CHAPTER 24

Months passed and the pregnant moms grew in size and hostilities, until baby shower celebrations began.

Rachel squirmed and tapped her mother's hand, "I think I'll take a walk. Baby's restless." Adinah turned her attention from Leah's shower festivities, and smiled at her youngest daughter. "Are you okay? Need help?"

Rachel laughed and rubbed her expanding belly. Soon the household would welcome her first child into the world. "No mom. I'm fine, but junior is restless, so a walk is in store. Besides, I did as promised. I participated in Leah's celebration."

Adinah frown just a little. "Yes, you did, and I appreciate the effort. Get some rest."

Rachel closed the patio door, easing quietly out of the house to take a stroll in her favorite part of the family gardens. Since childhood, this has been her secret place—one that no one else knew about. The sun was setting just beyond the trees. She breathed with relief, knowing that sunset meant Leah's loud, boisterous, gossipy girlfriends would be going home soon and her baby shower would finally be over. If Rachel didn't know any better, she would swear that Leah was keeping them around on purpose.

Leah deliberately sent baby shower invitations to her friends on a date prior to Rachel's celebration. Several of the guest had visibly yawned trying to send a signal it was time to wrap things up after that last slice of fig cake.

Only when the guests had gone, could the servants begin the cleanup, and be reassigned to prepare for Rachel's event the next day. She had grown weary of hearing about what this childbirth would mean for that fertile babymaker.

She glanced over her shoulder and saw Jacob watching. He followed as she moved beyond the pool area. What could he possibly want? In spite of the years between them, she still didn't know how he really felt about everything that had gone down. How did he feel about her family's deception? Had he lost any love for her?

After some distance from the house, he called to her softly. "Rachel." She turned stopped at the sound of his voice. Jacob opened his arms. "My Rachel, my love." Her knees nearly gave out, but she gathered her wits and ran toward the love of her life. Jacob grabbed her before she could take another step and covered her with his kisses. Then he repeated, "My Rachel."

Jacob and Rachel walked in the gardens for several minutes before sitting on one of the white iron decorative benches. Leaning on his shoulders, Rachel rubbed the neatly trimmed beard then gently turned to face him.

"Jacob, hear me. I have not been fertile in this marriage, so much so you have fathered now many children with only this first one belonging to me. As you have spoken, we prepare to leave my father's place to return to your country, soon after our baby is born. I pray that I may offer you more sons in years to come."

Jacob wrapped both arms around Rachel and hugged her close. "It doesn't matter what we've been through, how it happened, and the number of children I've fathered. Your baby will be special to me. You, Rachel, will always be the love of my life. Nothing can or will ever change that to the end of time. you are my girl."

A loud shout of laughter could be heard from the house, as Leah's "baby" celebration continued. Crying, she pushed him away. "Just listen to that. She and my father stole fourteen years Jacob, fourteen years of our lives. You came here, running from an injustice you did to your brother, Esau. You lied and deceived for an inheritance." Jacob started to speak, but she raised her hand as if she was stopping traffic.

"Please. For God's sake, don't say anything. I know all about it. There's been juicy conversations at my grandparents' home the short week while I was away several years ago. Gossip never dies Jacob. It may lie dormant for a little while, but it always comes to the surface. You can't run from it."

She stood and stepped back a few paces, so she could appraise him at a distance. "Then you come here, we fall in love, my father deceives you, and my sister and I become enemies. And so, began the turmoil that will never end." Rachel shrugged in defeat. "I was just collateral damage Jacob," she sobbed.

Looking sideways, pointing to the house in disgust, Rachel shouted in hopes her sister would hear. "Now she sits up in that house like a pompous queen bee celebrating the birth of your seventh child."

The tears flowed so heavily that she could barely see a few feet ahead. Jacob grabbed and embraced her again, gently rocking back and forth, smothering her with gentle kisses. "It's alright, my precious love. I am so sorry you have suffered, but we are together. We are one. My heart is, and shall ever, and always belong to you. No one else can replace the depth of my love for you—no distance, no time, neither wives or children, nor anyone else can separate or destroy my undying love for my Rachel."

The night breeze rustled Rachel's skirts as Jacob lifted and carried her to the gazebo overlooking her father's small vineyard. "Tomorrow is the beginning of our new normal. Soon we leave the past behind and begin a new life," he whispered. Jacob gently stroked her skin. "But tonight, I reaffirm to you before God. I take thee, Rachel, to be my one true wife from this day forward. Until death do us part. Nothing can or ever will separate us again."

COMMENTARY

In the Bible, the antagonism between these two sisters existed because each of them wanted what the other possessed. Rachel had the love of Jacob and Leah wanted that. Leah had baby after baby with Jacob, and Rachel—who was barren for almost a decade after marrying Jacob—wanted that.

They were blinded by envy, so much so, they never seemed to appreciate who they were or what they had. Instead of a life in which they could have supported one another by making peace with their situation, they chose instead to be miserable in their circumstance, oblivious to the fact that they had each been blessed by God.

Since having more than one wife in a household was a norm during those times, one has to wonder in what way Rachel and Leah could have benefited each other had their relationship been more palatable as sisters.

Before her marriage to Jacob, Rachel was a shepherdess. A shepherd is a person who guides or directs in a particular direction, as in tending or rearing sheep. This person watches over the sheep and, therefore, must have a keen eye to see any threats coming. This person also has to know the terrain, including best places for grazing, the different sheep and their bloodlines. They must also earn the respect of other shepherds. Sheep cannot live without the shepherd.

Clearly, from the description of a shepherd, though Leah was the oldest, her physical condition— "weak eyes" or "cross-eyed"— prevented her from having such an openly respected position among the tribe. We can safely assume this carried over to her marriage and management of the household of Jacob. Leah did, however, possess inner strength, humility, and perseverance, along with an unyielding loyalty to Jacob. This resulted in Leah giving birth to six sons, one of whom, Judah, who would form the tribe that would become the family bloodline of Jesus.

Rachel became the mother of two tribes because of her sons, Benjamin and Joseph. Joseph—of the "the coat of many colors"— gained renown for his position as one of the Pharaoh's officials due to his ability to accurately interpret Pharaoh's dreams. (Genesis 37, 39-45).

In spite of all the people, circumstances, and drama surrounding these two women, they both were blessed so they could fulfill their destiny and be a blessing to the world. (Genesis 29:17)

STORY FOUR: HOUSEWIFE OF SAMARIA: GOMER AND HOSEA

CHAPTER 25

"He let you hear his voice from heaven
so He could instruct you."
— Deuteronomy 4:36

"You can't seem to stop, can you?" a familiar voice shouted. "Still flaunting your hips and raising your skirts just enough to tease the men you pass in the marketplace. You don't even have the common decency to play your games when I'm not around to observe."

Diblaim balled his fist and shook them in the air, stepping close enough to his wife to strike. He stopped midway, whirled around, and slammed his hands on the table.

"No respect for me, your husband," he said through clenched teeth. "And now you've got our daughter, *my* Gomer, acting the same way—at her age. Her skirts are too short, flirting every chance she gets. Are you satisfied, you deceitful heifer? I should have tossed you out on your rump long ago."

Gomer opened her eyes, stretched and focused on the beam of light streaming through her window. She ignored the ragged, makeshift curtains her mother had sewed together out of scraps of old cloth. Instead, she pretended they were beautiful blue sheer drapes. She had been listening to the shouting for the last half hour. The topic never changed. Father would come home angry about something her mother did or didn't do with some man in the marketplace, at a friend's house, or on the road to somewhere. Always some man involved.

Gomer got one last good stretch before getting up to start her day. A door down the hallway slammed, and shortly after, her bedroom door swung wide open.

"Get your things together," her mother, Devorah, shouted, her thick reddish-brown hair flowing over her shoulders and dark brown eyes flashing with fire. "I'm out of here. We'll be staying at your Aunt Reba's for a while."

Gomer sat straight up in the bed. "Mom, for goodness sake. Moving to Aunt Reba's place?" She scrambled to gather her robe and slippers.

"She barely has room for her two kids and the dog. I won't have a room of my own," she blurted, half sobbing when she realized her mother was serious. "And we're going there now? Where will I put my things? I can't even take my cat because Aunt Reba has that scroungy dog."

Devorah took three giant steps to reach Gomer and grab her by the shoulders. Gripping hard, she raised her hand, ready to land a blow. In the middle of the act, she stopped, hugged her daughter hard, and cried.

"Fifteen years old and look where I have you," she said as she gripped one of the bed pillows and slammed it on the bedroom floor. "Don't you see? I can't live with your father anymore. He doesn't understand me. It's just too much trying to make this work. I need my space."

Wrapping both arms around her mother's neck, Gomer kissed her cheek.

"Mom, you don't have to keep calling Diblaim my father. We both know the truth. He's a nice man, but I'm not sure he's my father, and neither are you."

Devorah pushed away and locked eyes with Gomer. "What do you mean you're not sure he's your father?" she asked.

"It's okay." Gomer smiled, trying to hide her pain. "I don't need a father. I've got you."

"Of course, he's your father," Devorah said again without looking at her daughter.

Gomer shifted her position, adjusted the bed covers, then responded. "Mom, I've known the truth since I was twelve years old. You know Aunt Reba can't keep a secret. I found out one evening while I was at her place."

With a one-sided shrug, she fluffed the bed pillows and sat up. "You and father had gone out for the evening, and she'd been drinking good—I mean really good. I don't know how we got on the subject, but she told me about the other man in your life."

Devorah slid her hand in a circular motion over the bedcovers, concentrating on the creases. After a moment's silence, she muttered several curse words under her breath.

"She is so stupid. Always running her mouth."

Gomer patted her mom's hand while watching the tears slide slowly down her cheeks.

"I was going to tell you when you were older," Devorah said, heaving a deep sigh and lowering her head. "Really. I was."

She moved a stand of hair from Gomer's face. "I'm not sure, that's all. He could be your father but I'm just not sure."

Gomer shook her head, then hugged her mother hard. Removing the covers, she stood, opened the closet doors, and pulled down a large brown goat skin satchel.

"I'll start packing." She pulled several tunics from the closet, rolled and placed them in the bag, then turned to her mother.

"Might as well get started."

Wiping tears with the hem of her dress, her mother whispered. "It's going to get better, Gomer. You'll see. It's going to be much better living together with Reba—and maybe her occasional friend."

Devorah raised her arms, yawned and stretched, then walked to the door. She paused, looked over her shoulders, and smiled. "Besides, we're moving to a better life."

Gomer looked at her mother without smiling. Devorah raised her hand and shrugged.

"Well, okay." She said while scanning the room. "While your new room is not that much bigger, there will be enough space to ensure that you will have your own room."

Devorah opened the door, walked out, then stuck her head back in the room.

"Look. It's all temporary. All of this is temporary." Before Gomer could respond, the door closed.

Gomer sat on the edge of the bed, listening as her mother's footsteps faded toward the back of their tiny home. Scanning the room, she enjoyed the sudden peace and serenity her space provided. She focused on every detail of the room that had been hers for five years—the longest period of time she remembered living in one place. This would be the first move that would include only her and her mom.

"Well, at least that game is over," she mumbled. "Better finish packing." She got up and pulled an armload of clothes from the overstuffed space she called a closet. The familiar sound of someone playing a tune on her door with their knuckles made her pause and toss the garments haphazardly on the bed. Before she could reach the door, it opened, and in breezed her bubbly party partner and best friend.

"Hey, gurrrl," Sariya, whispered while shutting the door.

"Your dad told me you were in your room. I was hanging out the wash for my old lady and heard the commotion over here."

Jumping on Gomer's bed, Sariya sat, legs crossed, and chuckled. "I think half the neighborhood heard the noise. You know how quiet it was after the partying last night. I was just coming over to check on you, sis. What's up? What are they bickering about this time?"

Gomer flopped on the bed beside Sariya, with a sigh. "Wow, Moving," she said, while leaning her head back and searching the ceiling.

"Yep. We're moving, Sariya."

The cursing, insults, accusations, and screaming between her mother and the man she called father started again in the kitchen. Gomer glanced at her girlfriend, whose expression was blank and disinterested.

"Yeah, so apparently they're breaking up. It's just me and mom moving out, heading to live with Aunt Reba in Samaria."

Both girls sat silent for a moment.

"Listen." Gomer hugged her girlfriend tight.

"It won't be too far. We can still work on our plans to get a place together in a few years. We'll do much better than my mother and aunt ever did."

Gomer grabber her satchel and continued packing more of her things.

"You'll see. Just let me get settled, and we'll plan your regular visits. In the meantime, keep the marketplace games going just like we planned. Meet, flirt, tease and play."

They both laughed, then Gomer paused, and pointed at her friend.

"Remember. All trinket gifts are saved and traded for cash later. Bring home any cash you get for favors. Hide it and save it toward our moving plan. No deviations."

Nothing else needed to be said. Sariya stood and grabbed some of the clothes Gomer had thrown on the bed.

"Let me help you pack, but leave a few cute items out. Maybe we can get in a couple more money-making ventures before you leave."

They both laughed until the shouting and screaming between Gomer's mother and father began again.

CHAPTER 26

Gomer paused at the top of the hill, and appraised the long dirt and stone filled road leading to the cluster of houses on her street. She and her mother were now five years into their new life in Samaria, living with Aunt Reba. During this time, the girl Gomer had matured into a striking beauty. Her shapely body, accentuated by long slender legs, caught the eye of every man she passed—single or married. Connecting with the women of the night, Gomer gained expertise using various oils and coloring that enhance her body and the contours of her face. She had truly mastered the art of attracting the opposite sex, and took full advantage of her talent.

Though she enjoyed the last-minute invite to stop for a few cups of wine at her friend Rashad's favorite hangout after work, she didn't relish the walk home. The dusty trek required watching for unexpected holes in the path, and being cautious of dogs—both two and four legged. Gomer rubbed her ankle and tightened the strap of her sandal. With a deep breath, she entered the path, and walked the last leg of her journey home after a long day.

* * *

Reaching the house without incident, Gomer entered, removed her sandals, and walked in the kitchen area for a snack. Her mother was standing by the table, arms folded across her chest. "Where have you been?" Devorah shouted in a rough voice. "It's way pass midnight."

* * *

Gomer raised her hand in greeting. "Hey, Mom. What's the matter? I told you about the party a few days ago. Said I'd be late coming home from my job. So, I took a detour, and it's a little later than I planned." The corner of her eyes crinkled. "My goodness. You're acting like I'm ten, when I'm almost twenty years old now." She decided not to explain the invitation to the private party hosted by Rashad, a man with deep pockets and an even deeper appreciation for a girl with Gomer's skills. That information would open another conversation, leading to another one of her mother's lectures.

Throwing the sandals under a chair and grabbing a flask of water, Gomer leaned on the tall, cedarwood food prep table and anchored attention on her mother.

"This is a joke, right? You asking me where have I been. That's a question I've had for you for years. Is it that you didn't have a date tonight and now have an attitude?"

Taking a slow sip of water, Gomer eased onto the nearest chair, which wasn't nearly as comfortable as the one they had back home in Canaan. Aunt Reba certainly didn't put her money in décor. As expected, her father had made it clear they were only to take their clothes when they left. Nothing else.

"What's the issue?" Gomer protested, wiping a few drops of water that had spilled out of the flask. "Heck, you used to do all-nighters *all* the time. I remember trying to wait up for you. The morning sun would almost kiss the sky before I'd finally get to sleep, and you still wouldn't be home. So, Mom please. Let's cut the mess. My arriving home at this hour is nothing here in our quiet little town of Samaria."

While her mother was still fussing—mostly incoherently because she had been into the red wine so tough there probably wasn't anything left—Gomer left the common living space and made her way to the bedroom. The door closed, she stripped, grabbed her gown and prepared to refresh herself before bed. She opened the package of goodies she gathered from her night out. It had been a very busy evening with a special friend her mother didn't know existed. His wife didn't know Gomer existed, either.

As always, the night ended with her date showing appreciation for their intimate moment with an impressive financial gift and some jewelry, both of which Gomer hid in her undergarments until she was in the privacy of her room.

After securing her stash, among other items she had collected in an effort to get out from under her mother's thumb, Gomer grabbed her nightgown, closed the curtains to her window and got dressed for bed. She yearned for a long, uninterrupted sleep. Her girlfriend Sariya was arriving around noon to visit for a few days, and then the real fun would begin.

Before climbing in bed, she heard movement outside her door and a quick short knock before her Aunt Reba opened the door.

"Well, you finally got home, huh?" Aunt Reba gradually eased her way in, closing the door gently. "So, what's up?"

Gomer gave her aunt a cold look. "Well, let's see. It's three hours past midnight, I'm tired, and you didn't wait to let me welcome you into my space before entering. I'm missing the privacy of my old home."

Reba cleared a spot and sat on the bed, again without invitation, and ignored the remark. "Look, we need to talk, babe. Both your mother and I want you to take it slow in your choice of ... friends and relationships. We have plans to help you have a better life than we had."

Gomer's gaze narrowed on her slender, brassy-haired aunt. "What plans?"

"You know, fall in love, get married and have a decent chance for happiness."

She placed a hand over her heart and sighed.

"That won't happen if you're out here sleeping around and getting a negative reputation. There's already been some talk. You know I get all the gossip."

Gomer was standing by the wooden chest she used to store personal items, rubbing the handles to contain her impatience at having a woman who took on more male friends than her mother ever did tell how to live her life.

Grabbing her dress, she walked to her closet.

"I know what I want. Trust me, I've got this. I'm still young and want to have some fun while profiting from the experience." She smiled, taking in her aunt's sad facial expression.

"I'm not thinking about finding a husband right now. I definitely plan on letting these rich guys spend their money on me. Please don't worry. I know what I'm doing. I've had very good teachers."

Opening the door, Gomer pinned eyes on her aunt, and gestured toward the hallway. "If you're finished, I'm tired. I think we could both use some sleep before your next *friend* shows up."

Aunt Reba glared at her for several moments. "So it is," she said while rolling her eyes. She patted then pinched Gomer's hand gently before leaving the room.

* * *

"So, are you now the traffic monitor?" Sariya, laughed. Gomer hugged her buddy just arriving from her old home town.

"No, I was throwing out the wash water, looked up the road, and thought I saw your scrawny legs heading in this direction. You didn't walk from Canaan, did you?"

Sariya, threw her bags on the porch and sat on the steps. "No girl, but apparently drivers don't like coming down your road. They dropped me off by those trees up at the top of the hill, and refused to go further. Rubbing her feet, she laughed. Good thing I didn't pack too much.

Gomer shook her head. "Yeah, well. Some of the guys around here play it pretty rough. Sometimes they don't let the transport guys out of here unless they pay a fee. I thought they came to some arrangement with the drivers, but I guess some of them still don't trust it enough to take the chance."

"Listen kiddo," Sariya nudged her friend. "I've bout had enough of this sun. It's bright and hot. If we linger much longer out here, you'll have to carry me up these steps."

Gomer punched her buddy's arm. "Come on, let's get you settled."

She picked up Sariya's satchel and opened the front door. Before stepping inside, Gomer looked back and warned about the conditions of the house.

"I haven't been around for a few days, so it's a little messy until I can get things in order. Mom and Reba are the same. They only pick up trash or wash dishes when they are planning a party. Even then, it's hit or miss."

Devorah grabbed Sariya, as soon as she entered the house, and hugged her long and tight. "Hey little girl, she shouted. You are missed. Get in here and let us feed you." Gomer was surprised when her mother and

Reba pulled out bags full of grapes, figs, melons, and peaches. They ate, joked and laughed.

"Okay you guys, we've got plans for the night, and my buddy needs some rest," and pointed Sariya toward the hallway.

Devorah chimed in, as the girls headed for Gomer's room. "Okay. Ya'll get ya'll rest for your evening, but remember I expect to see you tomorrow before the sun rises tomorrow."

* * *

The girls maneuvered the small hallway to Gomer's room. "Hey, girlfriend. Put your stuff right here." Gomer gave Sariya a big hug.

"Like I said, we have a big night planned. There's a new place, we've been invited to visit a place where, lots of wealthy men go to escape their wives," Gomer laughed.

Sariya tossed her camel skin bag on the bed, stretched her arms over her head, and gave her friend the side-eye. "That's nice, but I hope there'll be some single ones too. I'm looking to catch me a husband."

Gomer laughed and ruffled Sariya's hair. "You're still working on *that* old plan, huh? Well, I don't care if they're married, single, young or old. I just need them to be free and loose with the money so I can tuck it away and cut loose from these depressing surroundings."

Gomer whirled around her small room several times, like a ballerina dancer. "When I get enough coins, I'll leave this place so far behind, and be no more than a memory, even to my mother. Though I think I'm just about an afterthought to her already."

Gomer stopped and reached for the bedroom door. "You look tired, kiddo. Put your bag on the floor and take a nap. We have a nice long evening ahead and I don't want you dragging like a rookie." She opened the door and looked back to see Sariya climbing under the covers on the side of the bed Gomer normally slept on. "By the way," she whispered. "Glad you made it here safe. See you in a couple of hours."

Gomer perched on the front steps of Aunt Reba's house. She didn't want to hang around the house waiting for Sariya to wake up so they could prepare for the partying they'd be doing that night. Based on the conversation with her mom earlier, the atmosphere was ripe for another argument that she knew would only end like all the others—bad. While brushing the dust from her dress, the front door opened.

Reba stepped out and quietly shut the door. "You're on the run again, girlie?"

Gomer didn't answer.

"Look," Reba offered. "I get it. You gotta plan to hit it rich, but you still need to pace yourself, kiddo. Me and your mom, we take it smooth and easy. You don't see us all out here in these streets."

Gomer looked at her aunt then kicked at the dust and shook her head. "Look, Aunt Reba, like I said before, I know what I want and how to get it." She grasped her aunt's hand in her own, softening her approach by saying, "Love you, but my tactics are fresher, more unique and sophisticated than yours or mom's, and it comes with a plan."

Reba heaved a heavy sigh and glared.

"You two focus on fun, a quick affair and some trinkets or favors. Then it's over till the next opportunity. I have a different set of ideas."

Gomer stood, adjusted her garment and smoothed her braided hair in place. "I'm going to hit it big and be well taken care of by somebody. Whether they're married or single. Now, I gotta go see if I can catch this guy I know. He's usually in the marketplace about this time of day. Need to make sure my plans are set for tonight." She gave her aunt a quick kiss and left.

"That girl," Reba mumbled while shaking her head. "Who knows? She just might make it."

* * *

Walking through the noisy marketplace, Gomer browsed through several stalls loaded with jewelry, beautiful linen and silk garments. The fragrances from a variety of perfumes and spices filled the air, coupled with music, laughter and lively chatter. Waving at several of the 'girls,' Gomer continued strolling—half shopping, half concentrating on the details of her plans for the evening.

Startled by the touch of hands encircling her waist from behind, Gomer struggled to pull away. She spun around, recognizing Alvon, one of the marketplace agitators, leaning closer, and grinning. He smelled of stale wine, and it was clear he needed a bath and some fresh clothes.

"Hey, Gomer," Alvon shouted, causing others to look their way. "I got something for ya. Come on over here." He pointed in the direction of a nearby building. Gomer pushed his arm away, ignored his comment, and proceeded toward another cloth maker's stall to browse the material.

Not to be ignored, Alvon caught up, stepped in front of her and stroked her arm before letting his hand slide down the side of her leg. "Hey, hey, pretty lady. Didn't you hear me?"

Gomer glared at Alvon then took two steps back, boiling with contempt toward this pesky fool who dared try to call her out in broad daylight. But before she could respond, she heard a deep, hostile voice behind her.

"I think the lady wants to be left alone," the Voice boomed, startling both Gomer and Alvon.

The stranger stepped forward to make his presence known. He wasn't very tall, but muscular. His face was rough and damaged from too much sun, but above that firm set jaw, his eyes were kind when he gazed at her. The man's eyes were firm and direct though when targeting Alvon, set as a warning not to move any further.

Alvon raised his hands like he'd been robbed. With a chuckle and a shrug, he walked away. "See you tonight at your favorite hangout, or should I say, dive, Ms. Gomer," he tossed over his shoulder.

Gomer never let anyone get one up on her, and she wasn't about to start now. She chased after Alvon and gave him a few choice, colorful words to think about.

By the time she returned to the cloth maker's stall, the stranger who had stepped in to help was gone. She scanned the area as far down as the end of the market stalls and even entered several of the sweet bread shelters to see if he had stepped inside, but he seemed to have just disappeared. She forced out a breath filled with frustration.

"Hey," she shouted to the man counting coins after handing a basket of cloth to a customer. "Did you see that guy who was just here?"

The stall owner raised his head quickly and snapped, "You mean Mr. Hosea?"

Gomer stepped closer. "Yes. Did you see where he went?"

The stall owner chuckled then responded, "Maybe perhaps he's going to the temple. He prays a lot you know." He stroked his wiry gray beard, looking Gomer up and down slowly. The corners of his mouth lifted into a wicked grin—until he cut his eyes over to his wife, who peered down her nose at Gomer.

"I don't think Mr. Hosea would be interested in the likes of you," the woman said in a disdainful tone. "You'd best go back to wherever you came from."

Gomer rolled her eyes and shook her head. "Amazing how everyone seems to know what's best for me." She picked up the sheath material she had considered buying earlier, flung it back on the counter, and kicked several pebbles it into the dirt before pushing through the crowd toward home.

Hosea stayed in the shadows and watched Gomer search the crowd for him. After his prayer time at the temple earlier that day, he left the sanctuary confused about what he felt—or feared—God was leading him to do. It was one of the most difficult times he had ever experienced.

"Seriously, Lord?" he'd said. "You want me to do what?" Hosea paced back and forth along the aisle at the front of the temple prayer area. Stopping, he clasped his hands, and dropped to his knees on the prayer rug. "Father God, hear me. How am I to do this thing? Me, marry a whore in order to show *your* love for Israel? Help me, oh Lord. This can't be. Send me a sign that I've heard wrong."

No matter how much Hosea bowed, prayed, and waited, he felt nothing that suggested he was not to pursue marrying a harlot.

After years of building the estate gifted to him by his parents, Hosea was certainly ready to marry and start a family. His dilemma was what he sensed as an undeniable *knowing* or *feeling*, the certainty that only happened when God spoke directly to his heart about what he was to do. He had been given an assignment to marry a woman of the streets—someone far below his station in life.

Before leaving the temple, he'd shared his thoughts with one of the leaders, Rabbi Berrei. The rabbi's response hadn't been as helpful to Hosea as he had hoped.

"Son," the Rabbi had offered "Israel is in trouble and in need of whatever you can do to assist. We all know you hear from the Lord, and

His ways are not always understood. I suggest you continue to pray and obey as you see fit, but always trust that God knows what is best and He will not let you down."

Hosea had left the temple on a mission to marry a harlot. His meeting and interacting with the woman Gomer had been part of the plan to find a harlot. He had already heard her name in the marketplace. After the confrontation with Alvon, he decided another day would be best—in hopes that he may have another message from the Lord before approaching the young woman.

Still watching from the shadows in the corner, Hosea felt a presence behind him. Preparing to defend himself from an attack, he whipped around to confront the unexpected visitor.

"Whoa! Hey, Hosea," Rashad said, holding up his hands to ward off the blow. "What's going on, man. How are you?"

Hosea smiled when he recognized his old friend.

Rashad looked around and asked, "What are you doing hiding out in the corner?"

Hosea didn't answer immediately. Instead, he grabbed Rashad's shoulder, embracing him while angling his friend's body to make sure that Gomer couldn't see him. "Good to see you. I'm just hanging out trying to plan my evening activities."

Rashad laughed and leaned on the wall. "Look no further. Why not join me and a few friends for dinner tonight?"

Hosea hesitated while watching the girl he helped earlier walk up the road. Rashad followed Hosea's gaze and grinned. "She'll be there. That's my ... friend, Gomer. Yeah, she's my good time girl. As a matter of fact, I saw both of you when that jerk approached her earlier. I would have stepped in to help, but I was in the middle of buying some items for my mother."

Hosea's eyebrow shot up, not believing a word of it. Men like Rashad didn't put themselves in harm's way for a woman like Gomer. That's why no one else intervened.

"Gomer's a lot of fun," he continued. "Like I said, I invited her to join us for a meal and a good time at my friend's place tonight. Of course, she thinks it's my place." He clasped a hand on Hosea's shoulder. "Don't worry. It'll be nice, man."

CHAPTER 27

Sariya greeted Gomer at the door of the house, munching on a mouthful of fruit and sweet bread. "Hey, where you been? I've been hanging out with your mom and aunt getting all the good gossip while you were Lord knows where, doing Lord knows what."

Gomer ignored her girlfriend. She grabbed one of her aunt's cushioned stools from the porch, brushed the dust off the seat, put it on the ground near the front steps, she kicked off her shoes and stretched. "Let's sit out here a minute. I need the fresh air."

Sariya looked around their surroundings. Several trash containers were overflowing two doors away. Someone had just thrown dirty wash water out of a window from a house across the road, and two cows just passed where they were sitting, with one of the beasts having dropped a pile less than ten feet away. Sariya smirked, "Uh, okay."

Gomer didn't miss her attitude. "Well, let's say the air is fresher out here than in the house. If I don't clean, it definitely doesn't get done. And I've been too busy to follow behind mom and Aunt Reba the last week or so."

Shifting her body as a way of changing the subject, Gomer scratched the steps with a stray pebble. "Actually, that's what I want to sit out here and talk to you about. It's time to make a move. I have some money saved like we planned. I just need to know how much you have toward the investment in our future. I've found several places just waiting for a deposit. We could be in our spot within a few days."

Sariya popped the remaining morsels of fruit and date nut bread in her mouth, then lowered her eyes and rubbed her hands. "Like I said, I've got some money, but shucks, Gomer, you know I had to pay to get here. Then, I couldn't come with those raggedy clothes I already had in my closet. Remember, you said we were going to some high-class places? Well, doing that cut even more into my savings. I thought I'd get a return on the investment with the first hit I'd make from our outing tonight and tomorrow. Sorry, but I'm in no position to make that kind of move just yet."

Gomer's heart sank. She was silent for a moment, thinking of how this would affect her bottom line. "Sariya, we've been hanging together for almost five years. You're my best friend and I love you, but I'm not going to spend the next year or two waiting for you to get your act together."

Sariya flinched.

"We had a real plan and I've certainly been doing my part by saving," Gomer snapped. "I don't have dates just for the fun of it. I canvas the place or listen to learn where a potential prospect is going to play for the night. Then I target that pigeon and work him the whole evening— overnight if necessary. My strategy is to come away with cash or enough trinkets to turn into cash. That's been my plan and it's the one you agreed to over 4 years ago."

Gomer threw a few rocks at the gift pile left by the cow. "See how that pebble is sinking into that stinking mess? If you haven't been following the plan, we worked so hard to create, then our future is also sinking in a stinking mess. We have to make some adjustments.

She allowed her friend to absorb those words.

"This is not my last stop," Gomer added, gesturing to her aunt's home. "This is their place. I don't plan to be living with two dried up party girls, hoping someone will stumble into this neighborhood and take me away. The only men who even come near this area barely have enough to pay their own rent every other week and take care of their families. I need to get out of here, and that's what I'm going to do."

Sariya fidgeted with the hem of her skirt. "You're right, of course. I need to do a better job, and I will. You'll see. I won't let you down."

Gomer patted her friend's hand. "It's alright, sis. I'll work it out. When I prosper, I'll make enough for both of us." She let the new plan settle in her mind a moment before reaching for Sariya's hand. "Now, let's go inside. I'm hungry and we need to decide what we're wearing tonight. This event is in one of the most affluent areas of the city." She tossed the stool to the side and grabbed Sariya's shoulder. "Come on, sweetie. Let's go prepare for our future."

CHAPTER 28

W hat do you mean you got invited to the North End?" Devorah shouted. She had just finished her fourth cup of wine and was feeling good. Aunt Reba was well beyond drunk. If it wasn't so pitiful, they would have been funny to watch. Instead, Gomer just felt disgusted.

She checked her satchel to make sure she had money for the transportation that had been arranged for the evening. Backing out of the room, she said, "You ladies enjoy yourself and I'll see you in the morning. I'll lock the door. Please just stay inside."

Gomer motioned for Sariya to head for the front door. Her mother nodded and mumbled something incoherent. Aunt Reba waved, but Gomer shook her head and focused on Sariya. "They'll forget we even had this conversation by tomorrow, and mom will have an attitude no matter what time we get in."

Peering around Sariya's head to see out the window, Gomer said, "Our ride's here. Let's go."

"Oh man, Gomer," Sariya said as they climbed into the horse- drawn carriage.

"Your friend sure sent us a nice ride. We'll be arriving in style for sure." She whispered so the driver couldn't hear their conversation.

Gomer smiled and tried not to seem too impressed, but she made a mental note to give Rashad a special hug for providing such classy transportation. They slowly passed the shabby houses, some shut tight and looking almost deserted, others filled with noise and people hanging outside looking poor and hopeless.

Gomer turned from the carriage window and sat back. She turned to Sariya and frowned. "If we don't get our act together, we'll be stuck in one of those places. Remember that."

"I never knew places like this existed." Sariya laughed and adjusted her attire while their ride followed a procession of other carriages up the winding driveway.

"You're right," she continued. "It's too far to walk, and it sure wouldn't have looked good for us to arrive on foot."

When Gomer's "date" Rashad had given Gomer money for the transportation, he'd emphasized she was not to spend the money on anything except the transportation he'd be sending. She was not to embarrass him by hiking up the long driveway.

Rashad was a rich playboy who had a different woman on his arm every night. His family was loaded—deep pockets. They had plans for him to marry a rich "prim and proper" girl from the right background and religion, but he preferred the slum side of town, where secrets stayed and the liquor and women came freely. He and Gomer started out as playmates, but eventually became friends. He promised her he would arrange for her to meet a good catch to support her, because he definitely planned to stay off the marriage hook. Afterward, she would have to make it on her own.

Gomer and Sariya stepped off the ride when it pulled in front of the mansion. "Wow!" Sariya chuckled while scanning the full length of the mansion. "So, this is a party place?"

Gomer paid the driver, then turned to Sariya. "It's a dinner club for rich guys and their women. Wait here." She walked to a blue and white canopied enclosure located just outside the building and lined with white candles. When she presented the attendant the envelope Rashad had given her, he waved her in.

She beckoned for Sariya to join her. "We're in!" Gomer smiled. "We're VIPs."

As soon as they entered the building, they were greeted by two men dressed in all white garments. One bowed quickly, gaze narrowing as he grimaced and looked at them suspiciously.

Forcing a tone of authority, Gomer announced, "We're guests of Rashad. Please direct us to his table."

The men straightened their stances immediately. "Oh yes," the bowing attendant replied respectfully. Please come. Your benefactor is right over here, ma'am. Follow me."

Gomer could feel curious gazes from the crowd following them as they moved past tables with women dressed in fine silk laced dresses and golden arm bracelets. Each table was arrayed with fine white linen. Large white candles laced in shimmering stone were in the center of tables full of platters with every variety of food imaginable including lamb, assortment of fish, grapes, figs, tomatoes, melon, roasted vegetables, honey buns, and a variety of other sweet breads.

The side bar tables, that surrounded the room, were loaded flasks filled with wine, fruit beverages, and water on the other whenever needed.

Gomer took a quick glance over her shoulder, and noticed Sariya struggling to pull down the hem of her dress, as if more fabric would magically appear to make it longer. Smiling, she dropped back next to her friend. "Sariya stop it," she said through her teeth. "You're fine. Let them look. Focus on what a great time we're about to have. Who knows? Your future husband could be right in this room, watching."

Sariya laughed. "Yeah, right." She pointed around the space. "This place is beautiful and very expensive. No matter what happens, I'm already having a great time."

The waiter opened two large doors. "Ma'am, the table is over here."

Gomer looked where the waiter pointed and saw Rashad rise and walk toward her, arms extended. "Gomer, my love. You made it."

They hugged and Gomer introduced Sariya.

"Come," Rashad said while wrapping his arms around Gomer's waist. "Let me introduce you to the group." Sariya glided along close behind, as Rashad went around the large square table introducing each one of his friends.

In the dim lighting, Gomer didn't recognize many faces in this new venue. "New prospects," she mumbled, then smiled and gave a relaxed nod to everyone she met.

Rashad led her to a man sitting in the corner. "Here is my reflective, have-to-drag-him-out-to-eat, childhood friend Hosea."

Gomer barely heard anything Rashad said. Focusing on the handsome guest. She blurted, "It's you! The man in the marketplace."

Gomer laughed. Hosea smiled.

CHAPTER 29

While adjusting her chair, Gomer studied her neighbor. Well-built, with a firm determined posture, Hosea was handsome. She noticed the same sunburned, rugged features that caught her attention in the marketplace earlier that day. His eyes were more intense then, but now they seemed welcoming and gentle, with just a hint of mystery that held her attention whenever she gazed at him. Through the evening, even when acknowledging greetings and comments from other guests, Gomer could feel his eyes on her.

"So, Ms. Gomer," Hosea interrupted as Gomer laughed at a comment from one of the guests. "I'd like to get to know you better, away from the marketplace."

Gomer stopped laughing and leaned on Hosea's arm. "You? Get to know me? Now that would be something. Be careful. You might get what you ask for."

Hosea touched her cheek gently, brushing her hair with several soft strokes. "You and me, Ms. Gomer. This moment is you and me," he smiled.

The evening was a wonderful blur. Gomer and Hosea dined on roasted lamb with delicate spices to enhance the flavors, and fresh vegetables all enhanced by great conversation. As the evening progressed, they created their own special world—conversing as if no one else was in the room. The only negative moments were when several of her "friends" stopped by the table to inquire about her availability after the dinner. She was nervous that one of them would make an inappropriate remark, or approach her with more familiarity than she wanted Hosea to notice. With his good looks and money, he was a real catch. She had no intentions of letting some horny bozo cause him to slip through her fingers.

Dinner had ended, and the mood and rhythm of the room transformed to a more clublike atmosphere. Judging Hosea's body language and tone when responding to her, it was apparent the change in music and room atmosphere was not to his liking.

Taking a long, slow sip of wine, she leaned closer to him and mused, "So, you don't drink?"

Hosea studied her face a moment, then smiled. "No. Is that a problem?"

Gomer cocked her head to one side. "Of course not," she laughed. "You don't mind if I do, do you?"

Hosea toyed with his glass of water before responding. "If that's what you feel you want, then you should have it."

He beckoned the waiter to bring the flask and pour more wine. Raising his glass of water to Gomer, he smiled and whispered, "Enjoy." He then took her hand and pressed it to his lips while studying her eyes. He placed her hand near the full glass of wine, pushed his chair away from the table, and stood. "I must leave."

Gomer was speechless and wide eyed. "Hosea, did I say something wrong? Why do you have to leave? The night is still young."

Hosea smiled again. It was genuine and warm, yet firm and resolute. "Come with me, Gomer. Let me take you to your home."

Gomer flushed with heat, despite the cool cross-breeze flowing in from the windows. She was genuinely caught off guard. She wasn't accustomed to this kind of treatment. Usually, if she left a place with a guy, it was to join him for an intimate moment. After the "meeting," she'd leave with enough money to pay for her ride home. Tonight, was different. This man actually wanted to take her to *her home*.

Gomer leaned back in her chair. "Yes, well I'm not alone. You see, Sariya came with me and I'm sure she's not ready."

Hosea leaned forward and took Gomer's chin in his hand. "I'll talk to Rashad. He'll ensure your friend is brought home safely." Kissing her gently on the lips, he whispered, "Gomer, come with me. It's time to start your new life."

CHAPTER 30

Hosea told Gomer to gather her things while he spoke to
Rashad.

When he returned, Gomer gave Sariya a hug, and
whispered, "No detours. Do I make myself clear? When this is over, it's
home. Do you hear me?"

Sariya smiled and shrugged. "Of course, home it is. I promise."

Gomer put her hand firmly on Sariya's shoulder. "It's no game out
here. You don't know these people and no one knows you. If you get
stranded, you'll have to make your way back to my place alone, and that's
not a good idea given the area I live in."

Gomer waved her arm around the space. "Look around. Trust me,
Sariya. Rashad will only offer once to make sure you have a ride. If you
show any signs of doing your own thing, he'll leave you to that decision.
Flirt all you want with these guys, even arrange to meet one or two of
them at the marketplace tomorrow. But make sure you accept that
arranged ride home when you leave here."

Sariya responded more seriously this time. "I got it. I will. Now go have fun."

Gomer gave Sariya one last warning look, as she and Hosea reached the exit to the dining room. What had once been a sophisticated restaurant was now transformed into a noisy, carefree party establishment. Liquored voices rose, and loud music quickly replaced the soft and easy atmosphere—all in preparation for dancing until dawn. Sariya stood and waved as Gomer exited.

"She'll be alright," Hosea said as he guided Gomer down the corridor toward the front entrance.

"I gave Rashad a few special instructions. And one of my manservants is posted on the outside, just in case. His assignment is to ensure your friend arrives home and to report to me if there are any issues."

Standing next to the open door, Hosea prompted, "Shall we leave?"

Gomer nodded and stepped into the warm night air. While standing together waiting patiently for their ride, Gomer turned to Hosea. "What did you mean back there when you told me it's time to start my new life?"

Hosea adjusted his linen garment, then brushed a strand of hair from Gomer's face before answering. "You're looking for something, and so am I. Perhaps we should join efforts and find what we're looking for together," he whispered. "Marry me. I can provide a comfortable life for you. Who knows? You might even grow to like my way of living."

Gomer stepped back from Hosea, as if appraising him for the first time, then laughed. "Marry you? Do you know who I am?" She put both hands on his face, smoothing his beard.

You're joking, right? I mean, you just want a pretend marriage, right?" Gomer leaned forward, massaged his shirt collar, and winked. Like you finding me a nice place to live, and you visiting any time you want to, right?"

Hosea shook his head. "No, I mean a wife, a *real* wife."

Gomer shook her head and smirked. "Now, why would I want to do that? Cleaning, cooking, housekeeping and making sure you look good. Uh, nope!"

Hosea laughed. "You wouldn't be doing any of that. I have maids and manservants to handle those duties. You would just let them know what you want."

Hosea moved closer to Gomer, giving her a look so intense it made her flush and clear her throat. He took her hand. "I have a good idea who you are and how you've lived. You see, I haven't lived a sheltered life." He brushed his lips against her forehead.

"I'm offering you an opportunity to adapt your lifestyle. Marry me, and enjoy a new adventure that may well help you live better."

The transportation arrived and Hosea turned to Gomer. "Don't answer now. Think about it." Taking her hand, he added, "Come, let me take you home."

The ride to Gomer's house was a quiet one. By this time of night, she was usually cuddling with her prey, negotiating gifts of money or trinkets, making arrangements, or extracting promises to meet in the marketplace to pick out a gift or receive money. This ride was different. As the carriage approached Gomer's street, she turned to Hosea. "Okay, you want to marry me, right?"

Hosea nodded.

"Then, yes. Why not?" she said. "It could be fun."

Gomer thought she saw a hint of sadness in Hosea's face before he smiled and patted her hand.

"Good," he responded. "This is good. All is as it should be."

Hosea hugged her close. "I'll arrange for the ceremony to take place within the week. In the meantime, no more travels to the marketplace alone. I'll assign a maidservant to stay with you temporarily until the ceremony. A comfortable pallet outside your door will be sufficient for her."

When Gomer eyed him. He adjusted in his seat and added. "Or she could sleep wherever else suits you. The point is the maidservant is to either go for you or with you, if you need to visit the marketplace before our ceremony."

Gomer kissed Hosea, before stepping off the carriage to enter her house. Hosea held her hand tightly for a brief moment.

"We won't have any fanfare over our marriage ceremony event, Gomer. It'll be a small, yet elegant ceremony with your family and, of course, your friend Sariya. You'll be pleased. Now, get some rest. I'll send word to you later today, should you wish to see me or should you have any concerns."

Gomer turned and smiled. "Or if you should change your mind?"

Hosea settled back on the carriage seat. "I won't change my mind, Gomer. I asked you to be my wife. I meant it when I asked, and I mean it now."

Gomer stood in the doorway watching Hosea's horse and carriage until there was nothing to observe, but a few flickering candle lights in several of the houses along the road.

Gomer entered the house, closed her eyes, and took a deep breath, as the front door shut. Her world was changing and she needed a moment to process the events. Except for the loud snoring coming from Aunt Reba's area, all was peaceful. Thoughts of how her life would be different, by being married to a man like Hosea, swirled through her mind. No waiting for Sariya to get her money together so they could move to a place where they would live more or less the same as her mother and aunt. One man. One home. The sound of that held a great deal of promise.

Moving past the clutter of clothes and stale, unemptied trash, to her room, Gomer undressed quickly and climbed into bed. Though determined to be awake, to share the good news when Sariya got in, she fell asleep before her friend was delivered home safe and sound.

"HEY, SLEEPY HEAD WAKE UP," SARIYA WHISPERED WHILE

pulling on Gomer's toes. "Wake up. Let's swap stories," she pressed, while squeezing in bed beside her buddy. "Since your guy whisked you away so fast, I'm sure you have much to tell."

Gomer turned over, stretched then leaned on one elbow to face Sariya. "Maybe I should start with the end. Pulling Sariya closer she whispered, "I'm getting married."

Silence, then laughter. "You're doing what?" Sariya poked Gomer in the arm. "You? When? And to whom pray tell? Only Rashad can handle you."

She shared the details of her evening and ended with, "I said yes."

Sariya jumped off the bed, almost knocking the wash pail, on the nightstand, to the floor. "Are you crazy? You meet the guy and, in one, day you agree to marry him?"

Gomer laughed, laid flat on her back, and put both hands behind her neck. "Correction, my dear friend. I met this rich, well respected, gentleman. He liked what he saw, meets *my specifications*— according to *my plan* of getting out of this hole. He asked me to marry him, and I said yes."

Sariya adjusted the covers, but didn't respond.

Gomer hugged her girlfriend tight. "Don't worry. I won't shut you out.

Let me get settled, and we'll see what we can do about you." She grabbed the covers, turned her back, and dug deep in the pillows.

"Now, go to sleep. I need my rest. Tomorrow I'll have to tell mom and Aunt Reba that their in-house cook, housekeeper and message- runner is no longer at their disposal. That in itself is going to be a hot mess."

CHAPTER 31

After seeing Gomer home, Hosea had the carriage driver drop him off at the temple and wait. He entered the synagogue and fell on his face before the Lord.

"Father God," he prayed, "I'm doing as you asked. I'm marrying a harlot. I'm here today, Lord, to ask that you close this door if it's not your will that I do this. I need to hear from you, Lord God, very soon, if I have misunderstood your instruction that I am to marry a woman of the street."

Hosea waited over an hour, lying face down on the prayer rug. "Lord, are you there? I need to hear from you." Getting on his knees and raising both hands toward heaven, pleading his case. "Did I hear you right, Lord? Or, did I get this wrong? I'm about to marry this harlot. You told me to do it, right? I need confirmation again that it was you."

He waited a few more moments. The room lighting was dim. Hosea could faintly hear a dog barking in the distance. A cool, soft breeze blew and moved the curtains at the window just beyond the altar, but he heard nothing else. He felt nothing, during his prayer time, that convinced him it was a mistake to marry Gomer. Hosea believed, in *His* silence, God had spoken.

Rising from the floor, brushing the dust from his clothes, Hosea stepped off the prayer rug, resigned that he would marry the woman Gomer.

While he paused at the door of the temple, the carriage driver approached him. With a bow, he announced "Sir, may I know when you're able to leave? We have another assigned transport, and I would need to make arrangements for you if you are staying longer."

Hosea fell silent for a moment, half regretting the use of outside transportation for the night, but it was necessary to prevent household servants from knowing where he was going. Rashad's parties were not something he frequented, and he wanted to eliminate unnecessary servant-to-servant gossip.

Hosea nodded to the driver. "I'm ready." Without looking back, he left the temple and boarded the transport for home, to make arrangements for a God-ordained, covenant ceremony of marriage to the beautiful harlot Gomer, a woman he barely knew.

Hosea did not expect to find his home lit with candles, nor the level of activity that appeared outside his home when he arrived. It was some minutes before he recognized the familiar face of his father's manservant, carrying several bags into the quarters. The manservant, Reuben, waved, then bowed.

"Your parents are here, sir. They have only just arrived."

As Reuben proceeded to bring the last of the guest satchels from the caravan, he directed Hosea to the location of the guests.

"Your father and mother are having light refreshments in the dining room, sir, before retiring." Hosea nodded and smiled, then proceeded into his home without another word. When he reached the door, he paused. Though not used very often, this was one of his favorite rooms. The rich, colorful tapestry, polished shittim wood table and chairs, and candles mounted in brass holders were all gifts from his mother, who spent much time putting items in order. Taking a deep breath, he focused on giving an enthusiastic, warm greeting. Hosea turned the knob and entered the room.

"Father, mother, what a pleasant surprise," he said while scanning their faces. Hosea walked to the dining table, embraced his mother, then stood at attention. His father was not one for any physical expressions of emotion during a greeting.

"I know I have been writing you about my prayers these last few weeks, and about my belief that the Lord has instructed me to demonstrate His love for Israel by marrying a harlot." Hosea opened his arms, palms up then clasped his hands behind his back. "I have truly appreciated your patience and silence, as I worked through this process. I realize it has not been easy for you." Stepping back from the table, Hosea paced the floor, rubbing his hands.

"In the note that I sent recently about plans to marry within these next few weeks, I didn't expect either of you to travel here for a ceremony. It wasn't necessary. As I wrote, I am completing what I believe I have been assigned to do. The initial steps in this process were to visit various places, make my choice, and perform the marriage immediately. It so happens I've completed that task, and made my selection. This was not a normal boy meets girl, falls in love, plans a wedding kind situation. I've prayed, heard from the Lord, and am proceeding."

Hosea stopped pacing and stood before his mother. "I do admit, however, this woman I selected to will marry is different. I believe there are redeeming qualities in her, and I did offer to arrange a small ceremony, so that her mother and friend might attend. She's—"

Hosea's mother, Shoshanah, raised her hand and shouted. "Stop, just stop." She threw her napkin down and arose from the table.

"Please don't repeat what you wrote to us in one or two your notes. We're here to get you to understand what you're doing not only to yourself but to the family. We never thought you'd be so uncaring. Of all the nice girls you could have selected, you chose a whore. There are no redeeming qualities with this decision. What in the world is going on with you?"

Hosea's father, Beeri, moved from the table and put his arm around his wife. "Enough, Shoshanah. We agreed this would be a civil conversation." He turned to Hosea.

"Son, we have concerns about the way you have been processing things lately, and have come to offer support. We thought we might talk more about it, and help you reach a better decision."

Hosea was silent for some minutes. His father and mother returned to their places at the table. They sat quiet, waiting. Hosea clasped his hands together, in prayer motion, and placed them on his mouth. He looked up for a brief second, before gazing on his parents.

"Father, though I understand your concern, there is little you or mother can do to change the situation. Though you are welcome, I don't expect either of you to attend the ceremonies. but I do ask, however, that you respect my decision, as I intend to proceed as planned."

His mother covered her eyes with both hands and cried. His father sat very still for a moment, watching his son, then stood and helped his wife out of her seat.

"We'll rest tonight and leave in the morning. I'll pray for you, my son. But we will have nothing to do with the marriage ceremony or your wife."

Hosea bowed to his parents. "I fully understand your decision father. We'll speak of it no further. If you'll excuse me now, I'll see to your comfort for the night." Hosea left the room. The only sound that could be heard was his mother crying.

His parents left for their home long before he arrived for breakfast the next morning. He ate the morning meal in silence, alone with his thoughts.

CHAPTER 32

"Mother, I'm not going to repeat this. You are not inviting your girlfriends to my wedding. It's not that kind of party. You and Aunt Reba are my only guests. And no, you won't need any male escorts. Your boyfriends can stay home. I'll see to it that you both are picked up and returned to the house when the festivities are over."

Aunt Reba peered in the kitchen, laughed, grabbed an apple and took a bite. "Starting fireworks early huh?" Getting no response, she eased into a chair.

Her mother cut her eyes at Gomer, then started pacing the floor. "So, you're about to walk into the best opportunity of your life and have no intentions of taking care of your mother or your aunt, right? All I'm asking is to have a few close friends *observe* the ceremonies, enjoy the delicacies I'm sure will be on hand, and maybe meet some of these rich folks."

Moving closer to Gomer, arms flailing in the air, Devorah squeezed her eyes shut and gritted teeth. "Look. You'd think I was trying to bring a disease in the place. What is it with you? Too good for us now?"

Gomer stood erect, giving full eye contact, while speaking as calmly as she could. "Mother, I have always contributed to life here, and I intend that you are comfortable—*here*. You've made a choice about how you live. I made a choice about how I'll live. The two worlds no longer meet. I'm getting *married*. The fact that you two have chosen to live your life this way doesn't mean I can't live a level up. What happens when the beauty fades? What happens when the parade of lovers run out?"

She reached for her purse. "You and Aunt Reba are invited, but on my terms."

Gomer ignored the hostile silence while handing her mother a slip of paper with a name and directions.

"Here's the place you and Aunt Reba will go to be measured for the outfit I want you both to wear. You can pick any of the designs on the list. I selected the colors, length of dress and limited cleavage exposure."

Looking from one to the other. "There will be none of your regular low-cut fashions for this wedding."

Moving toward the door, Gomer paused, looking directly at her mother. She half smiled. "Mom, please be happy for me and do what I ask. Sariya and I have to go. I have a fitting. I'm getting married in less than a week, so I need you to go to the marketplace today. Hosea has ensured that you'll receive high priority services."

"Look at you," Devorah snarled. "Trying to be important. Even your speech has changed."

Something that could have been pain slashed across Gomer's heart. "If you can't or don't want to do this, let me know now."

Silence followed her last comment. Gomer smiled, bowed to her mom, and left the room.

Waiting on the steps outside the house for the arrival of Hosea's new maidservant and the carriage for the trip to the marketplace, Sariya giggled. "You're really following directions, aren't you? You know, the instructions Hosea gave you to go to the marketplace and pick the material for your wedding gown—after he sends the maidservant," Sariya teased.

"Cut it out," Gomer responded with a warning look, weary of all the sly remarks from her friend. Their transport arrived, and she nodded a greeting to the maidservant. Pushing Sariya aboard, she quipped, "let's go select my very expensive wedding dress material."

The wedding ceremony was all that Gomer could imagine. Held at her new home, Hosea ensured the ceremony and celebration room were decorated in the opulence that fit her new station in life as his wife. A grumpy Rashard was on hand as the best man, and Sariya, as maid of honor. Gomer's one regret was that only a small number of guests were invited to attend.

Gomer chose to walk down the short path alone. She had no idea where her father was, and no interest in his walking with her down the aisle, even if she had discovered his new location in time.

To her disappointment, her mother charmed Hosea into connecting her with two of his rich friends as escorts—one for herself and the other for Aunt Reba. They made a complete spectacle of themselves with food and drink, but the other guests seemed to tolerate the loud chatter and "expressive" overly-suggestive dancing.

Sariya, attempting to console Gomer, whispered, "Just ignore it, sis. This is the last time you have to put up with making excuses for your mom and Aunt Reba. I'll make sure they arrive home—alone— but she's going to have a whopping headache after all that wine tonight."

Gomer hugged her girlfriend, who finally seemed to get over her jealousy. "Thanks, sweetie. I'm sending one of the maidservants over in the morning to deliver some groceries and clean the house. You know that my room is yours until I can figure out how to get you here with me. Hosea is nice, but I think he won't take too kindly to me inviting a guest so soon."

Rashad crossed the room and asked, "May I have a dance with the bride?"

She obliged.

An excellent dancer, he whirled Gomer around the room with ease, all the while commenting on how beautiful she looked. Then he snarled, "This life isn't for you, Gomer. I give it a year and you'll be back in the club with me and the rest of the men who have ... sampled what you have to offer. Hosea is a nice guy and all, but he won't be able to keep up with your needs."

Gomer waited for the dance to end before responding to her former lover. "You talk too much, Rashad. I like where I am and can handle doing whatever I need to do to keep it. That includes making Hosea happy. Very happy."

Rashad bowed, clearly not happy at this turn of events. "Let me take you back to your husband, but remember, I'm just a messenger away when you get tired of this married little rich girl game. Or when he realizes that he can't turn a harlot into a housewife."

By the time midnight approached, all the guests were fed and happy. Congratulations ended, and everybody took their leave.

Hosea and Gomer stood in the celebration hall alone.

Hosea took Gomer in his arms and gently kissed her. Before she could offer a comment, he placed his finger on her lips. "Tonight, our marriage truly begins, Gomer. There will be many new changes for you."

Moving her toward the dessert table, he offered her a piece of nutcake. "I saw you with Rashad, and he's been dropping little hints of things. I'm here to help, to show you this life. But you must want this new way of living, and be willing to let go of your old ways."

Gomer slid a piece of honey bun between Hosea's lips. Giving her husband the side eye, she unbuttoned the collar of his tunic and smoothed the hair below his neckline, and smiled. "Before we go over my new instructions, let's go play house, starting in the bedroom, to seal this marriage covenant. The rest will come in due time, my husband." She pulled him closer. "All in due time."

CHAPTER 33

"After all this time, you can't seem to stop, can you?" Hosea shouted so loud, servant conversations nearby trickled to a halt. "Still flaunting your hips and raising your skirts just enough to tease the men you pass in the marketplace. Nothing matters to you. Not even how our children feel or your responsibility to have respect in the community. I've tried to give you every opportunity to be a wife and mother—gave you everything you could ever want or need. But it's just not enough, is it?"

Gomer chuckled, dismissed him with a wave. Over ten years and two kids, and Hosea was still trying to get his wife to transform from the old, and step into a better life. Despite of constant forgiving misdeeds and praying, she rejected his beliefs and remained the same.

Leaning against a table, toying with a goblet, Gomer responded. "This is too funny. Seems like I remember listening to this scenario years ago, when my father was in a heated argument with my mom." Pouring wine from the flask on the dining table, she saluted her husband before drinking. "I wonder if the kids are listening to our conversation now. Wonder what they're thinking?"

Pushing the flask out of the way, she sauntered toward Hosea. "Look, I never promised you anything more than what you got—me in all my glory. I never bother you about your work, your prayers, your God, and your worshipping in the temple. Never asked you to change your life for me," she yelled, ignoring his murmurs. "I tried it your way, but it was too boring. And let's not pretend you didn't know what you were getting. So, let's stop playing wounded warrior, shall we?"

Hosea grabbed Gomer, holding her tight to control the struggling. "The one thing I've always been clear about, Gomer, is knowing what I was getting when I married you. I thought ... prayed that when we had children, you would make an effort to change your behavior for them, if not for me. I can see now that was a dream wasted."

Shoving her, Hosea brushed his hands. "I have to be away for a while. I arranged for you to have a vacation, my sweet Gomer. You will be kept away from the marketplace and all your late-night gathering spots. They're now off limits." Eyeing her in disgust, he pointed his finger. Per my instructions, you'll not be allowed use the carriage to leave the estate for any reason. Your movements will be monitored. In my absence, you'll have time to be a mother and reflect on how to become more like a respectable wife." Hosea's jaw dropped, but she said nothing.

Without another word, Hosea opened the dining area door. Before exiting, he dropped his head, stood very still for a moment, then looked in her direction. "When I return, we'll talk." Hosea excited, leaving a fuming Gomer behind.

"What's your issue, Gomer?" Sariya laughed and took another bite of her fig cake, while eyeing other delectable items on the lunch tray.

"So, you have to remain on the estate with the sounds of a waterfall in this private pool we've been enjoying, lush gardens, being waited on hand and foot, with no real kid duties. Do you know how many women would kill for the privilege to have the wonderful life you're living? You sure get worked up over some real dumb mess."

Sariya pulled her chair closer to Gomer and tapped her face. "Wake up, sis. Is it so bad married to a rich guy and a being mother too?! From what I can see, you've got some pretty sweet kids."

Gomer smiled but didn't agree with a word she said. "You like it, huh? Well, why don't you try it on for size? I've been in this jail for a week now. Let's get serious. I need you to do me a favor. Visit Rashad when you leave here."

She handed Sariya a small sheet of parchment paper. "Tell him to come to me tonight just after dark. The details of my plan are outlined in the note."

Sariya glanced at the information, stood, grabbed her pouch, and moved toward the exit.

"Forget it Gomer. You're not dragging me into this. You made your bed, and from my point of view, it's a nice bed. You have to walk this out on your own. You haven't asked about me lately. So busy lamenting over your horrible life. But I'm making it—actually met a nice guy myself. I'm going to make it work."

Shaking her finger in Gomer's direction, Sariya moved closer to her best friend. "I suggest you do whatever you can to make your choice more bearable. There's no going back, but the way forward is up to you. You need to get off the fence, Gomer."

Sariya looked around the veranda, then shrugged. "I'll check on you in a few weeks to see what you decided."

Gomer jumped from her chair and pulled a handful of Sariya's hair and held firm. "Look. I've done a lot for you. The only reason you met this nice guy of yours is that I allowed you to stay t my house, *in my bedroom*, while I made sure the rent was paid. I haven't asked you for a shekel in all these years. Yes, you've been there for me through the childbirths and scuffles I've had with Hosea. But make no mistake, you owe me." She shoved her onto a chair.

Sariya was silent as she gathered her things. "OK Gomer, you're right. You have helped me. So, I'll take your note to Rashad. But I'm never coming back. I won't help you make an even bigger mess of your life. You'll have to do it without me from now on."

Sariya touched her friend's cheek. "You're still my sister. If you have a change of heart and realize this is your best life, you know where I am."

Sariya left her friend, sitting by the pool.

Gomer slumped forward in her chair. She had reached an impasse. She would have to make her way back to the lifestyle she loved on her own.

Gomer was pulling the fifth outfit from her closet when the handmaid knocked and entered. "Excuse me, Ma'am. A gentleman is here to see you. He said you asked him to come."

Gomer smiled. "Have him seated in the guest area, and pull both of my satchels down from the closet. I want them packed with as many of my clothes as possible. Do you understand?"

The handmaid nodded and proceeded toward the closet. Gomer checked her hair, smoothed her dress, and went to the guest area to receive Rashad. She strolled through the hall toward the staircase leading to the front lobby. It was truly a beautiful home. With torches glowing, the marble floors shimmered. The details of the tapestry set off the rich tone of the décor. She would miss this, but nothing else— not even the kids.

Gomer entered the guest receiving area and rushed to Rashad's arms. "I've missed you so much. It's dreadful here. Take me away."

Rashad hugged her close, then pulled back. "Whoa. Wait a minute. Does this mean my princess is finally bored?"

He stepped back a few paces and smiled. "I told you this wouldn't work, but I gotta hand it to you for making it this far. Just don't know what you want me to do now. You know I'm not the marrying kind."

Gomer walked to the sideboard and reached for two cups and the flask of wine. She poured both to the rim and handed one to Rashad. "Help me get away. I need to leave now, before I change my mind again. I have never accepted his God or his life. I need to breathe again."

Rashad moved closer to Gomer, ran his hand down the side of her leg and kissed her neck. "Okay, so coming to me periodically isn't enough. Now you want to run away altogether. Let it be so. I leave tomorrow for the countryside estate of my parents a few hundred miles north of here."

Gomer pushed back. "I can't do that. How would you explain me to your parents?"

Rashad laughed. "Kind of funny, you worrying about what people think." He stepped closer, breathing, then licking her ear.

"Relax," he whispered. "They won't be there. I'm going for some fun and relaxation with friends. You can join me while you decide on your next move."

Gomer laughed, grabbed Rashad, and kissed him passionately. "Oh, yes. That would be perfect. I'm having my things packed now."

Gomer had been in her room for over an hour when Rashad sent word that he had grown tired of waiting. She was to come with him now.

"Take these satchels to the coach outside," she instructed her handmaid. "Tell the gentleman I'll be there shortly."

Gomer quickened her pace down the hall toward her escape. Before leaving the upper level, she opened the door to her children's room. They were sleeping soundly. She smiled as she contemplated telling Rashad that one of the children may possibly be his, but thought it best to leave that detail alone. Closing the door, she rushed down the steps to the exit.

Rashad waited for her to be settled in the carriage. "This is your moment, my love. There's no turning back once we begin the journey." Rashad grasped her chin firmly. Look at me. "Are you sure you want to do this?"

Gomer smiled and touched his thigh. "Let's go. I'm already feeling a weight lifting. It's such a relief."

Rashad directed the carriage drive to move. Silence filled the house, as several of the servants stood at the door, watching. The moon was full on this evening, illuminating the path of yet another detour in Gomer's life. She never looked back. Not one tear of regret. It was finished.

COMMENTARY

Histstory does not reveal whether Gomer ever found real happiness. As a wife, she lived a life of unfaithfulness, despite Hosea constantly providing her needs, taking her back when she wanted to return, and forgiving her over and over again. When in trouble because of poor decisions, Hosea was there to bail her out—even buying her back when she sold herself into slavery after the men, she ran with had used her up and left her destitute and starving on the streets.

There has been mention of the possibility there were three Gomers represented in the story. From this author's point of view, Gomer was one person represented in three stages of her life, which was based on a transitional process many women may take to survive situations not of their making.

In her youth, Gomer was born to a lifestyle that was acceptable to the one person she felt closest to—her mother. We can only imagine her survival techniques in an environment that required adapting and following acceptable behaviors, without question, so that she was not abandoned along the way. This is Gomer number one, the person Hosea married.

Gomer number two is the second phase of her transitional growth. She has some years of experience manipulating and applying her "work around the issue" processes on her husband. Hosea believed it was his assignment to marry and exhibit the biblical attributes of the fruit of the Spirit—love, joy, peace, longsuffering, gentleness, goodness, and faith.

Gomer number three was seasoned in her bitterness, had no use for learning what God could have been in her life, and lived with a "you do you, and I'll do me" attitude. She was born with her purpose already connected to Hosea. Prophetic rebellion and rejection of God was the standard.

The biblical account of this story demonstrates the correlation of a husband's love for his wife, and God's love for Israel. In spite of her behavior and rejection of the faith, Hosea forgave Gomer repeatedly—rescuing her from choices that took her to the depths of disgrace, including multiple partners and selling herself into slavery. Israel's rebellious behavior, bad choices and disbelief led them to terrible situations; but God, in His love, forgave over and over again. Long- suffering was Hosea's burden until he divorced Gomer for her infidelity and continued to preach and encourage others to return to the Lord.

ABOUT THE BIBLICAL FICTION SERIES

Don't miss the remaining three upcoming standalone series, covering men and women of the Bible whose lives transformed the world.

BOOK 2 – THE BACHELORETTES OF THE BIBLE

The Bachelorettes of the Bible is fictional journey that explores what could have been the behind scenes life of some of the most well-known Bachelorettes of the Bible.

Rahab was *no doubting Thomas*. Yes, a harlot of circumstance has a story. She didn't challenge the power and influence of God. Clearly, something happened in this woman's life that would lead her to have such confidence that she would save a "chosen" people from slaughter when they were spies and considered enemies of her people. No wonder, she would negotiate a way to be given favor for herself and family.

Delilah was *the first female barber* and she did her job all too well. Delilah's survival techniques came out of living a life of planning, patience, and practicing proven strategies as a business woman. When one move failed, she didn't give up. She simply changed her strategy. This woman used the most powerful weapon known to man to win the battle of the will. Who was she really? What brought her to this level of influence? The story that proves an ultimate warrior, in spite of his armor, can be overpowered by the plans and will of the ultimate seductress.

Rizpath Even a *concubine can influence the heart* of a king—not by pleading—but feeling empowered to perform a vigil oversight protection of her sons. What if we could envision the past experiences of her life that created a strong, determined woman who chose to stand guard at the base of seven bodies hanging on trees. How did she make a decision that created the situation which saved

Israel from famine? The journey of a female slave positioned as a guard at the gate.

The Ten Virgins Speaking of the worst-case scenario of what it means to be *"a day late and a dollar short,"* here we have the story of ten virgins, five who are prepared for the coming of the bridegroom and five who are not. Our God is a comedian and this story has a lighter side that reminds us not to allow procrastination to creep in so that our light becomes dim because we have not been "self-pruning" the wick of our lives. The behind the scenes view of becoming a "Lamp Trimmer," ready when called.

BOOK 3 - THE BACHELORS OF THE BIBLE

Endless Love will never be played in the lives of these Bachelors who chose to follow a cause rather than build their lives with wife and family.

The question is what cause could create such a choice. In other words, who are these guys?

Jeremiah *"The Town Crier,"* Jeremiah earned his reputation as a weeping prophet, constantly expressing messages of hope and warning of pending disasters because people weren't following rules and laws. What a label. Was anybody listening or was he just an annoyance? What was it like interacting with him when he was outside of his priestly household? Imagine how this young man might have been viewed by the average person in his time, and how he might have responded. We'll explore, behind the scenes, the possible life of a boy turned prophet whose words were eventually "like fire, shut up in his bones."

Elijah *"Setting the example,"* Elijah was a trail blazer, with numerous mandates established to him by God. The best overall description is a man who, with much attitude, had great impact on situations "all over the place." Elijah kept it real. When he was confident, he rocked. When fearful, he "rolled out," and expressed his doubt and fear openly to his closest friend, God. With what appears a deliberate decision not to include wife or children in his life, this is a behind the scenes "what if" exploration of the reclusive man on his "exclusive" journey through some of the situations he faced.

Daniel *"The first lion tamer,"* Daniel was a king's servant kept close to the throne because of his ability to interpret dreams and understand visions. What could this young man have really been thinking when he fulfilled his mission to stand in a den of lions and enter a fiery furnace? Defying the odds and supporting his friends, he walked unscathed. This fictional review explores what could have been Daniel's state of mind, when some people thought he "lost his mind," as he strolled toward his challenge?"

Lazarus *"The brother in the middle,"* Imagine three adult siblings still living together. Lazarus is a bachelor living with his two spinster sisters. With a scenario like this, "what a friend we have in Jesus," might have been his favorite song had it been known during that time. Add to this the fact that one of his sisters is Martha—the oldest sibling—and we now have an interesting family dynamic to explore.

BOOK 4 – THE REAL HUSBANDS OF THE BIBLE

Paying the cost to be the boss is the best description for husbands of the Bible. In a time when actions speak louder than words, no matter what the influence, here's another view of men, in course of history, accepting "the buck stops here."

Ahab and Jezebel These two were the *"Bonnie and Clyde"* of the Bible. The uniqueness of this marriage was how one fed diabolical behavior to the other. Jezebel, in her actions, had no use for "Wives, submit yourselves to your own husbands as you do to the Lord. For the husband is the head of the wife (Ep 5 22:23) ..." Ahab found strength in her disobedience and lack of respect. The key ingredient to failure was the role of the husband, the king. As in Bonnie and Clyde, she led, he followed. This is a "what if" view of this team's backstory that could have had a different ending.

Aquilla and Priscilla *"And the two became one."* Aquila and Priscilla are an example of the marriage covenant in action. These two people made their living together, grew together, worshipped together and risked their lives to serve a key prophet of the word. This is one of the original husband and wife business owner teams. Their story demonstrates how two bold, ambitious, and courageous people can partner in a successful marriage journey. There is always a team, behind the scenes, traveling with and helping a prophet. Aquilla and Priscilla are one of those teams, and we are going to explore their journey "up close and personal."

Ananias and Sapphira *"The case of the ultimate smack down."* Nobody does it better. These two people traveled a road to inevitable destruction by following a pattern of a car traveling a one-way street, with the ultimate dead-end leading to an immoveable wall. Something in their individual character makeup brought them together, opening doors to their making the wrong decisions leading to their ultimate death. Significant here is Ananias dies first, which means he led the way. This story explores what brought them to the choice that led to death.

Elkanah and Hannah *"Performing in a three-ring circus,"* this is a story of how a man managed two wives, one of whom became the mother of the prophet Samuel. After ten years with one woman, Elkanah chose to add a new wife. Why? Because he could. Unfortunately, his choice created a pattern of juggling relationships between two women who had a passionate rivalry for his attention with dangerous consequences.

AUTHOR BIO

Theresa V. Wilson, M.Ed., CPBA is an award-winning suspense/thriller Screenplay Writer, Indie Book Entrepreneur and fiction and non-fiction author.

An ordained minister, former educator and nonprofit executive, Theresa has been involved in her writing passion for over twenty-five years. Her experiences include serving as faculty member and newsletter editor for the American Christian Writers Association, and founder/coach of a writers' group. Always exploring, she has written and published poetry, created an audio CD, and achieved several awards for her screenplays. As one of TBN's latest authors, Theresa expanded horizons to include television commercial advertisement, under the Trinity Broadcast Network.

Theresa's nonfiction titles include *When Your Normal Is Upset: Living Secure in Uncertain Times*, *The Writers' Guide to Achieving Success: A Workbook for Implementing the Plan*, and *Reaching, Searching, and Seeking: Letting the Spirit Lead*.

Her screenplay, *Out of the Mist: The Battle in the Middle Realm* received Award Winner status from Los Angeles Motion Picture Festival, Independent Shorts and Global Shorts, and Award-Winning status at ScreenPower Film Festival, United Kingdom, Independent Shorts and 13Horror.com Film Festival, and placed finalist in the California

Women's Screenplay Festival. Theresa lives with her husband, Doug, in Owings Mills, Maryland.

For Speaking Engagements and Media Inquiries:
theresa@theresawilsonbooks.com

For more information about the series, visit:
www.theresawilsonbooks.com/the-real-housewives-of-the-bible

 facebook.com/WritersCoach21

twitter.com/WritersCoach21

 instagram.com/TheRealHousewivesofBible

CPSIA information can be obtained
at www.ICGtesting.com
Printed in the USA
LVHW021456041120
670707LV00009B/1048